His Dad Will Do

ANNA KENSING

KENSING BOOKS

Cover design: Natasha Snow Designs

www.natashasnowdesigns.com

Editing: Jen Sharon

ISBN: 978-1-959268-03-1 (ebook)

ISBN: 978-1-959268-05-5 (paperback)

One

SILAS

THEY SAY REVENGE is a dish best served cold and I guess that's apt, because I am fucking freezing.

The mesh shirt and tight jeans I'm wearing are supposed to leave little to the imagination, but a blast of frigid air blows a scuffle of dead, brown leaves across my shoes and my balls shrink up into my stomach.

My nipples are hard, but again, from the cold, not so much from anticipation or arousal. I'm standing on the front steps of my ex-boyfriend's dad's house and I'm here for a reason.

I'm here to seduce him. Because Lance always bitches about how his dad only fucks twinks way younger than him, and I can't think of a better "fuck you" response to what Lance did to me than to be the latest twink in his dad's bed.

I'm wearing a coat, of course, because it's December in Connecticut. But the coat is this long, black velvet thing that's like a cross between an old-fashioned smoking jacket and a trench coat. The kind of coat I wear to the clubs to look hot in, not to stay warm in. And anyway, doing up the buttons will only cover up my chest and I'm supposed to be looking irresistibly sexy.

Even though I'm rethinking whether this was the best or worst idea I've ever had.

It's definitely the ballsiest, despite the current state of my balls. So before the rest of my nerve freezes over and falls off like my dick is about to, I ring Logan Reynolds's doorbell.

It's just past eight o'clock on a Friday evening and Logan is home, thank god. Warm light spills from the huge living room windows. He's alone, too, it seems like. There's no extra car parked in the driveway in front of the closed two-car garage or on the street in front of the large house.

Because that would just be the icing on the humiliation cake —if I've taken a Metro-North train all the way to Westport, Connecticut to seduce my ex-boyfriend's father and said father already has a Grindr hookup in his bed.

The front door is mostly glass, so I see Logan cross the open floor plan of the living room and kitchen to answer. Between the brightness of the interior lights on his side and the moonless night outside, I don't think he can tell who's standing on the other side of his door, and I know he's not expecting me. So his surprised expression when he pulls the door open isn't... well, surprising. He fills the doorway, his broad shoulders almost brushing the frame, and my dick gives an interested twitch, despite the cold.

"Silas? Are you all right?"

Now that I'm actually here, I'm not exactly sure what to say, despite all my anticipation and planning. I look down at his feet, which are bare, despite the winter chill, and then up at his face under the fall of my bangs. It's a look that used to work on his son, the rat bastard, and I'm hoping like son, like father. "Um..." I start, like an idiot.

"Of course not, what was I thinking?" Logan swings the door wide. "Come in, son."

The house is blessedly warm, thanks in part to the fire in the double-sided gas fireplace that divides the living room from the dining room. I shrug my coat off and shake my hands out, opening and closing my fists to bring the blood back into my fingertips.

Logan takes my coat and tosses it on a peg in the entryway, then tilts his head to look at my face. Chloe says I've got "come hither" eyes—whatever the fuck that means—but Lance also once said they were the first thing he noticed about me, so I use them to the fullest extent on his dad. They're green, with flecks of gold in them, and I've smudged the barest hint of eyeliner around them to really make them pop. My lashes are long and thick and I legit bat them at Logan, whose own eyes narrow at me.

He's in his late forties, twenty-five years older than me, and he is rocking that silver fox look like nobody's business. His expression shutters, like the stone-faced lawyer he is. But he also looks down at my chest. At the piercings in my nipples visible through the mesh shirt, and then briefly lower, before he drags his eyes back up to my face.

"No," he says, and the firm tone of his voice makes my dick twitch.

"You don't even know what I came here for."

His eyes flick up and down my body again and he crosses his arms over his chest. "I'm not blind, Silas. And I said no the last time, remember?"

The last time is totally why I came here tonight.

Even if, to be honest, I don't remember a lot of it.

I remember attending the annual holiday party at Logan's law firm. Logan had invited me and Lance because a lot of his clients are Broadway producers and he knows about my dream to someday have a musical produced on Broadway. I remember agreeing to meet Lance there instead of arriving with him. Because Lance said he had to work up until the party started to get ahead on a project.

Well, he got head, all right. By a cater-waiter in an empty office at his dad's law firm. Where I caught him when I was coming back to the party from the john.

The next thing I remember is getting super drunk and Logan pouring me into a taxi. He got in next to me and rode the entire way from his office in midtown Manhattan to

Chloe's apartment in Brooklyn after I screamed in the middle of Seventh Avenue that I was never going back to the condo that Lance and I have been sharing for the last year.

"I remember your dick didn't say no the last time," I say. I step closer to him. Close enough that my chest almost touches his. He's a few inches taller than me, and I have to tilt my head up to meet his gaze. He's just standing there, his face impassive, his eyes boring into mine.

To his credit, he doesn't deny what happened. How when the cab swung around a corner a little too fast and I fell against him, he put his arm around me. How when I laid my head in his lap—initially to block out the endless streams of light shining through the cab windows because they were making me dizzy in my drunken state and I was trying not to puke— his erection rose under his black wool suit pants.

How he spread his thighs wider when I nuzzled my face into his crotch. How he stroked my back while I exhaled a steady stream of hot breath against his hardening dick.

Until the taxi reached Chloe's apartment building and Logan lifted me off his lap, leaned forward and murmured to the cabbie that he'd be right back. He hustled me up the walk and propped me up against the brick front of her building, then turned me over to Chloe when she answered the bell, with a terse, "His boyfriend cheated on him and he's exceedingly drunk. He needs someone to take care of him tonight."

Instead, he says now, "Well then, it's lucky for both of us that my dick doesn't make my decisions."

"Is it?" I lift one hand and drag it down my own chest until I reach my crotch. "What if we both got lucky tonight?"

I cup my hardening dick in my hand, through my jeans, and the back of my hand brushes against the soft lounge pants that Logan's wearing. There's an answering hardness under his pants, but he still hasn't moved closer to me.

Or farther away.

"Silas." Logan's voice is low and rough. He swallows and I track the movement of his throat under the scruff of his close-shaved beard. "You were drunk."

"So drunk," I agree. I stroke my cock through my jeans, which causes the back of my hand to rub against his cock, too. "Didn't change what I wanted then. And I'm not drunk now."

"You just caught your boyfriend cheating on you, Silas. Less than a week ago. You need time to get over him."

I slow the movement of my hand. Dragging it gently, so very slowly, along the ridge of my erection. Barely brushing over his at the same time. His cock twitches and strains toward mine.

"You know what? I don't think I do." I don't want to talk about Lance, because if I do, I'm likely to say things about him that will ruin any chance I have of getting what I came here for.

Logan's hands clench into fists at his sides. He's got broad hands with big knuckles, the kind of hands you'd expect to see on, like, a construction worker or a gardener. Not a corporate lawyer at a white-shoe law firm with a prime address in mid-town Manhattan. I imagine Logan's hand holding the fat Mont Blanc fountain pen I've seen him use when I've stayed over here with Lance. Then I imagine his hand wrapped around my cock and shiver.

One hand opens and lifts a little, like he's about to touch me, but then he drops it again and wipes his palm on the side of his lounge pants. "Silas. Even if I did have a natural reaction to you in the taxi, you were dating my son."

His hand closes into another fist, then opens again. "What kind of asshole would I be if I took advantage of you?"

I shift a tiny bit forward, so that line of my jeans-covered cock brushes against his jutting out under his loose pants. "I'm not dating your son anymore. We're completely over. I'm a free agent."

I don't know if that's the right analogy—I'm not into sports, like at all—but whatever works, right?

Logan's eyes drill into mine. I feel like a witness on the stand in a trial for everything that matters to me. "And you wouldn't be taking advantage of me. You'd just be giving me what I'm asking for."

I reach for Logan's hand and lift it to my chest, pressing his palm over my right nipple. I sway forward so he can feel my nipple ring against his palm and my dick against his.

"What are you asking me for, Silas?"

"Isn't it obvious?" I give a tiny thrust of my hips. Logan's hand tightens over my pec. I'm asking him to fuck me. And suck me and let me suck him and do all kinds of other dirty things to me.

"Your boyfriend—my son—just cheated on you with another man."

"I'm negative, if that's what you're worried about." I got tested the morning after the party, in a flurry of fear and betrayal and rage. And then again yesterday, in anticipation of what I was planning.

"I'm negative and on PrEP," Logan says. Oh. I didn't know he was on PrEP. Will he fuck me bare, then? Because that would be awesome. "But that's not the point," he continues.

"What's the point?" I ask.

"The point is...we can't, Silas." But his palm is kind of grinding into my chest, twisting over my nipple in a way that feels freaking amazing. And he lifts his other hand so that he's cupping my jaw. His thumb strokes my cheekbone and I lean a little into his hand.

"Why not? You want me, don't you?" I know he does. The taxi wasn't the first time I've seen Logan have a "natural reaction" to me. "You can have me."

"Silas," he starts, but he's still twisting my nipple ring. "For one thing, you're the same age as my son."

"Younger, actually," I tell him. "I skipped a year in elementary school." I'm twenty-two and have spent the eight months since I graduated from college trying to get the musical I wrote as my senior project staged. And waiting tables. A lot of waiting tables, to be honest.

"Jesus," Logan says and his voice is a little shaky, but his hands are firm on my body.

"Want me to call you Daddy, then?"

Those are the magic words, apparently, because Logan's eyes go even darker and the hand cupping my jaw slips down to tighten around my throat. He squeezes just enough to constrict my breathing, but not so much to cut the blood flow to my brain. All my blood runs south anyway, and my dick is throbbing harder than it ever has in my life.

"Do you even know what you're saying, boy?"

Of course I know. I've watched my fair share of porn—more than, probably. I've tagged along with Chloe to the kink club she frequents for newbie night and I've done a lot of research into the Daddy/boy lifestyle. It's something I've thought about exploring.

Not with Lance, though. Not even once. Which probably says almost as much about why our relationship failed as him cheating on me.

Because it's something that I've been thinking about more and more lately. Having a Daddy. Being a boy to a strong, firm Daddy who will take care of me the way no one ever has. I don't know for sure whether Logan's into the scene, but a few things Lance has said about his dad makes me think it's a possibility.

More than a possibility, if Logan's hand around my throat is any indication. He tightens his fingers just a little more, but not so much that I can't take in enough breath to say, "I want you to fuck me. *Daddy*."

Two

LOGAN

JESUS FUCKING CHRIST. This boy in front of me. Writhing under my hands, staring up at me with those indecently long lashes, those come hither eyes, and that fuckable mouth.

My son's boyfriend.

Ex-boyfriend, a part of me helpfully reminds me. The part of me that wants to push him to his knees and feed him my cock. The cock that's hard enough to pound nails and is begging for something firmer than the soft, glancing touches the back of his hand had given it moments ago.

I can't believe Lance cheated on him. I mean, I can believe it. He's my kid, but he can be a selfish, inconsiderate bastard sometimes. He's a lot like his mother, who I accidentally knocked up in a drunken, last-ditch experiment with heterosexuality during my senior year of college. She refused to consider an abortion, but then dropped Lance on my doorstep when he was six months old and took off for the backpacking trip around Europe that the pregnancy had delayed. She lives in Paris, works as one of the lead designers in the fashion house she'd briefly modeled for.

Lance thinks I didn't know about the ever-changing parade of boys he fooled around with in high school while "studying" or "watching movies" or "playing video games." Playing with as many joysticks as he could get his hands on, more like. Also a lot like his mother.

Silas was the first guy Lance brought home as his boyfriend, and I admit that I found Silas attractive from the moment he walked into my house. He's exactly the type I go for in my hookups. But they seemed to really like each other and I'd hoped that Lance was finally settling down.

So, I ignored my inappropriate attraction to my son's boyfriend and made him feel welcome in as fatherly a way as I could muster. They've been dating for a couple of years and moved in together when they graduated from college. Shit, it's Lance's trust fund that bought the apartment they live in. Obviously, it's Silas who will have to move out now.

But that's a problem for later. Right now, Silas is here, in my house, with my hand around his throat and my fingers plucking at his nipple ring. He gives a low moan when I tug gently on the bead threaded through the ring. The contrast between the cool metal of the hoop and the heat of his skin pushes all thoughts of Silas's living situation out of my head.

Lance is a damned fool to let this boy go.

But if he really has let Silas go…

"Are you sure?" I let go of him too, at least to give him a chance to rethink this. "You don't have to do this just to get back at Lance. In fact…" I take a small step back, to give him some space, but I can't resist running my fingers through his hair. I brush the blond strands back from his forehead and tuck them behind his ear. "You shouldn't do this just to get back at him."

"It's not only that," Silas says. He ducks his head and glances up at me under the fall of his hair, which has drifted down over his face. Again. "I mean, yeah, I want to get back at him. But I've wanted you for ages." He takes a deep breath. "Even when I was with him. You want me too, don't you?"

He blinks those sinfully long lashes at me, and for Christ's sake, this is deeply fucked up. What the hell was he doing with

Lance if all along he wanted me? I feel a twinge of guilt at the idea of my son's boyfriend fantasizing about me when he was supposed to be in love with Lance.

But no more than a twinge. Fuck it. Lance had his chance with Silas and he fucked it up. Now I get my turn.

And I will not fuck it up.

One more thing, though. "You don't have to call me Daddy." I can't deny how much I want him to, but he doesn't need to know that. It's fucked up enough that he wants to take revenge against Lance like this, and even more fucked up that I'm letting him. Because I'm not sure I can take it if he only does it for revenge and not for real.

Silas looks uncertain for the first time since he arrived. He bites his lower lip and Jesus fuck, I want to be the one who bites it. But I hold back and wait for him to decide whether we're really doing this.

"Okay," he says. "Now will you fuck me?"

I lunge for him. I wrap one arm around his waist and the other around his shoulders. He lets out a little squeal when I pull him flush against my body and our erections rub against each other. "Not so fast, b..." I clamp my lips shut.

Christ, not ten seconds after telling him he doesn't have to call me *Daddy*, I almost call him *boy*. This is going to be harder than I thought.

His lips curve up but before he says anything, I dip my head and kiss him. I'd planned to start slow and gentle, but Silas doesn't seem to want slow and gentle. His mouth opens immediately and his tongue is tangling with mine and it's all wet, hot, gasping lips and tongues and breath. He's got a tongue ring, and oh fuck, I wonder how many other piercings he has. I revel in his sheer enthusiasm and bend him backward, pressing my hips against his and plundering his mouth.

I pull back after a few minutes of scorching kisses and try to calm myself. Because if we're really going to do this, it won't be a quick hand job standing up in the foyer. Silas sways toward me, his lips still parted, and I put one hand on the middle of his chest to keep him from reaching for me. The mesh of his shirt is cool and silky under my palm, but his skin is hot underneath.

"That's enough for now," I tell him. He nods and his throat works as he swallows. The rush of him listening to me—obeying me—even in this tiny instance makes my head light.

I move into the open living room space, close the lid on my laptop and move it from the coffee table to the kitchen island, along with the draft contract I was reviewing before Silas knocked on my door. I fold my reading glasses and set them on my laptop and Silas makes a small noise, still standing in the foyer, waiting for my instructions.

I look over at him and he's staring at me with wide eyes, his mouth open a little. "Put them on?" It's a tentative request and his cheeks go pink after he says it.

He looks down at his feet, then past the kitchen where Lance's bedroom and the guest room are. "I saw you wearing them one night. I'd come out for a glass of water and you were in here, working late or something. I don't know why it's so hot —you wearing reading glasses—but I stood in the hall for like, five full minutes, just watching you while you were reading."

I remember that night. I'd been reading a series of court decisions, making notes about how they applied to my client's case, when some movement just past the kitchen caught my eye. Silas hovering in the hall that leads to Lance's bedroom, staring at me. His hair was rumpled—from sleep or having just fucked my son, not that the reason was any of my business—and he was wearing only a T-shirt and a pair of SAXX boxer briefs. The briefs had loud orange, blue, and pink stripes, and as he stood there, watching me, the pouch at the front slowly bulged.

Neither of us said anything until Silas finally muttered something that sounded like, "'Night, Mr. Reynolds," and I went to bed that night with a raging hard-on for my son's boyfriend. It wasn't the first or last time.

I slowly unfold my glasses and settle them on my face. Silas smiles. "You look like a proper Daddy now."

I don't need the glasses to see how hard he is. Tonight he's wearing black jeans so tight they look painted on and the buttons of his fly strain to contain him. I move to the sofa and sit down. I have to spread my legs to make room for my own hard cock, but I ignore that for the moment.

To cool down, I take a sip of the Manhattan I'd made myself shortly before Silas knocked on my door. I hold the liquid in my mouth for a few breaths, letting the whiskey seep into my membranes. Liquid courage, I suppose.

"Come here, Silas."

Silas comes toward the sofa and, instead of sitting on it next to me, he pulls the coffee table back and drops to his knees at my feet, resting his ass on his heels. He peeks into my cocktail glass and fishes the maraschino cherry out with his fingers, pops it in his mouth, and rolls it around ostentatiously, then draws his lips back to show the cherry between his teeth. He bites down and cherry juice drips down his lips and chin.

He kneels up, which puts him close enough that his chest is almost brushing my knees, and lifts his chin, offering his lips to me. I lick the sweet juice from his lips and chin and he moans. "I want you to come on my face and lick it up, just like that," he says.

Oh, fuck yes, I will do that. First things first, though.

"Take your shirt off," I tell him and he grabs the hem and whips it off. His chest is pale and hairless and his collar bones stand out starkly. His nipples are rosy pink and the rings are colored like a rainbow, with captive green balls. I take one in each hand and tug at them gently. His head tilts back and his nipples tighten.

"You like that?"

He's panting now and swallows before answering. "Yeah."

I tug a little harder. Silas moans. "Do you have any other piercings? Besides the tongue ring, I mean?"

He looks at me and his face is flushed. "You'll have to get me naked and find out, won't you?"

I flick my fingernails at his nipples so the rings bounce up and down. "Naughty boy. Come up here."

He gets to his feet and I lean back against the sofa. I gesture to my lap and he straddles me, then goes to unbutton his jeans. I pull his hands away. "Not yet," I say and drape his arms around my shoulders.

I stroke my hands down his sides and around his back. My hands nearly span the width of him and his skin is smooth silk stretched over lean muscles. I lift him up enough to get my mouth around one nipple and Silas tangles his fingers in my hair.

"Oh god, yeah," he breathes, as I suck his nipple into my mouth and use my tongue to play with the ring. He's writhing in my arms, his hard cock rubbing against my chest, and I've still got the other nipple to take care of.

When I take that one into my mouth, Silas's squirming increases and his fingers are clenching and tugging at my hair. "Logan," he says shakily. "I think I'm gonna...oh shit, don't stop, but I could..."

I let go of his nipple and he whines. "Come like that?" I ask and catch one of the green beads in my teeth. "Has Lance ever made you come just from playing with your nipples?"

I shouldn't ask that question, but I've always wondered about Silas and Lance's sex life. All the times they've stayed overnight here—holidays and summer weekends so they could use the pool—and I've never once heard noises coming from their bedroom.

And yet, Silas is full of noises tonight. With me.

"Nooo," Silas moans. "He doesn't like his nipples played with, so he doesn't think about playing with mine. And he doesn't like the piercings. He thinks the rings are trashy. So, he doesn't even touch them anymore."

My son is an inconsiderate fool.

I lift Silas a bit higher and get my mouth back on his nipple. He's twenty-two. If he comes now, he'll be hard again in minutes. And this boy deserves a lover who makes him come as many times as possible.

Three

SILAS

OH MY FUCKING god. I play with my own nipples when I masturbate and I love tugging on the rings—it's why I got them pierced in the first place—but I've never come from just nipple play before.

Logan is alternating between my nipples, licking, sucking, tugging at the rings, and I can vaguely hear my own voice letting out a stream of moans and curses. I don't even know what I'm saying, but it's definitely not stop.

I'm going to blow my load and I'm not even all the way naked. Logan isn't even touching my dick. But there's like a line of gunpowder from my nipples direct to my nuts and every nibble, tug, and flick of Logan's tongue or teeth sets it on fire.

Then Logan bites down gently, just behind the ring at the base of a nipple and I can't hold back anymore. My cock jerks and I think I shout something and I'm pressing Logan's head to my chest and squirming on his lap and then I'm coming in my pants like when I was dry-humping Peter MacKenzie at a sleepover when I was fourteen.

Logan holds me through it and I'm quivering and shaking. He's licking gently at the tip of one nipple, then the other, and back again. Until I slump against his chest in a boneless heap.

"Stay," I hear in a quiet whisper against my ear.

"Mmmm?" I don't have the energy to lift my head, which is resting on Logan's shoulder. Logan's arms are still around me and he's stroking up and down my back.

"Stay the weekend. Let me make you come as many times as I can. How's that for revenge?"

I muster up the strength to sit up and look at him. He's still wearing his reading glasses, the lenses now smeared and smudged from the sweat currently drying on my skin. He looks serious. And...cautious, maybe.

Like he's afraid I'll say no, now that I've come and maybe I'm not thinking with my dick anymore.

I look over my shoulder at his laptop and the pile of papers he moved from the sofa to the kitchen island. "Don't you have work to do this weekend?" Lance always said his dad is a workaholic and hardly ever takes weekends off.

He shrugs his shoulders. "Nothing that won't keep. Just some research I was going to do, but I'll have one of my associates do it next week."

Logan represents high-profile clients in the entertainment industry. Broadway producers and Hollywood executives planning to film movies in New York City and people like that. The kind of people who also don't take weekends off.

But if he's willing to put all that aside for me, then yeah. And if he can make me come so hard just from playing with my nipples, then I've got to know what it would be like to have him fuck me. Still...

"What if Lance comes to visit?"

Another shrug. "Why would he?"

Because Christmas is next week and Lance always goes to his dad's house for Christmas. I drop my eyes to somewhere in the middle of his chest. His T-shirt is rumpled from where I was leaning against him and I tug it smooth. "Have you, um, talked to him? Since, I mean?"

Since the holiday party, I mean. Because I wasn't the only one who caught Lance in the act. While I was standing in the doorway of that darkened office, trying to figure out if I was really seeing what I thought I was seeing, I heard Logan's voice behind me. "Boys, I want to introduce you to…oh, Jesus, what the fuck?"

I don't know what happened between Lance and his dad and whoever the fuck was blowing Lance at his dad's law firm holiday party. I made a beeline straight to the open bar and downed two, maybe three, glasses of Jameson and ginger. After getting a good look at my face, the bartender the firm hired had the decency to go heavy on the Jameson and light on the ginger ale.

An older guy with sandy blond hair noticed me and asked if I was all right. I think I was about to tell him just how very fucking far from all right I was when Logan materialized at my elbow, my coat draped over his arm. "Sorry for the interruption, James, but I need to steal Silas away for a minute."

James—whoever he was—raised an eyebrow at Logan, then nodded at me. "Take care, kid," I think he said, but by then, I was completely trashed. Everything else until I was with Logan in the cab is a blur.

"No," Logan says now. "I haven't talked to Lance since the party." There's a beat of silence and I realize that I've been plucking at Logan's T-shirt. "Do you want me to?"

I don't want Logan to confront Lance for me, that's for sure. Definitely not now, while I'm half-naked in his dad's lap, who just promised to make me come all weekend.

On the other hand, the whole point of seducing Logan was to get revenge against Lance. And what kind of revenge would it be if he never finds out? Because now I'm picturing Lance walking into his dad's house on Christmas Eve to find me snuggled up next to his dad in front of the tree and the look of shock on his face gives me a dangerously heady sense of delight.

But surely Logan won't want Lance to know what he's done with me.

Logan brings a hand in between us and circles my nipple with a broad finger. They're super-sensitive now and I let out a totally undignified squeak. He chuckles and moves his hand down to the waistband of my jeans. The front is soaked with come and distinctly cold and clammy now.

He pops the first button and holy fuck, I'm getting hard again. It's been, like, three minutes since the best orgasm I've had in a long time and my dick doesn't think that's enough.

"Come on, baby," Logan whispers, and his fingers undo the second button of my fly. "You're all wet and messy. Let me clean you up and take care of you."

I let my eyes close and my shoulders relax as Logan finishes unbuttoning my fly. "Yes, Daddy," I whisper. "I'll stay." Fuck Lance. He wanted a blow job from a random stranger. I'm going to get one from his dad. And more.

"Good boy," he says. He kisses my cheek and a delicious curl of want grows in my chest and stomach. It's so dirty, calling my ex-boyfriend's father Daddy. And while I'm sitting in his lap covered in my own come, too.

But when he calls me a good boy, it's not just my dick that responds. And that's gonna be a problem, if I'm catching feelings for Lance's dad.

Logan shifts me from his lap to the sofa next to him. He pushes me onto my back and lifts first one foot, then the other, to get my shoes off. He lets them drop on the floor next to the sofa and returns to the waistband of my jeans, which he slowly peels down my legs and off, then tosses over the coffee table. He strips my socks off, tosses them away, too, then brackets my hips with his large, warm hands.

"These were the ones you were wearing that night," he says.

They are. They're my favorite pair of SAXX underwear and you better believe I wore them tonight. I wanted him to remember that night I stood out in the hallway, looking at him in his reading glasses. Getting hard just at the sight of him, looking so serious with his brow furrowed in concentration on the cases he was reading. His big hand holding that fat Mont Blanc fountain pen, scrawling notes on a legal pad balanced on the arm of the chair he was sitting in.

I had to jerk off in the guest bathroom before I went back to Lance's childhood bedroom. Luckily, he was asleep and never knew that I'd gotten off imagining his dad letting me suck his dick while he read his legal papers.

The bright colored stripes on the fabric of my underwear are darkened now from my come staining them. Logan peels them off me as slowly and carefully as he did my jeans and my cock bobs free and stands straight up, waving hello to him.

He's still fully clothed—still with his reading glasses on—and I'm naked. Sprawled across the sofa in the house Lance grew up in, with his dad spreading my legs apart and running his hands up the inside of my thighs.

"Jesus Christ," he says, in a low voice that teeters between concern and arousal. "When the hell did you do that?" His hands bracket my groin and his thumbs brush my balls in a way that makes me squirm.

"In the spring," I say. I've got a Prince Albert piercing through the head of my dick and a ladder of curved barbells on the underside of the shaft. Sort of a graduation present to myself.

Logan is staring down at my dick with his mouth slightly open and my hips lift up, my cock straining for his mouth. He licks his lips, but spreads his hands wider and presses my hips down.

"I thought about you while I was getting them," I whisper.

His eyes flick up to my face and back down to my dick, like he can't stop looking at it. He presses his hands firmly on my hips, wordlessly telling me to keep still.

I do.

He brings his hands close enough together to gently cradle my dick and strokes upward, his palms barely skimming my shaft. His thumbs rub lightly over the ladder of piercings and it is fucking torture to keep my hips from thrusting up to get more friction.

But I'm good. I want to be his good boy—I want him to tell me I'm his good boy—so I keep still, like he wants.

"Did it hurt?" Crap, his voice has more concern than heat in it now, though his eyes are still eating me up and his cheeks are flushed above his close beard.

"Like a bitch when the needles were going in," I admit. "But then it just ached a little while they healed." Logan is still skimming his hands up and down my shaft, and his thumbs are still delicately tracing over the curved barbells and the little balls at each end of them. I've got six of them through my shaft, plus the Prince Albert, and I picked anodized titanium for the ladder balls in rainbow colors, ending with a white pearl at the tip of my dick.

"They're all healed now," I add. "You don't have to worry about touching them."

Please touch them, Daddy.

Logan's eyes flick back up to mine again and this time, he looks at me for a long moment. His thumbs rub a little more at the piercings and I keep my eyes on his while letting out a low moan.

"You thought about me while you were getting them?" His look sharpens. "Not Lance?"

My skin is on fire and I can feel a drop of precome dripping down my shaft. Logan's whispery touches are driving me crazy, but so is the hard look of possession that's dawning over his face.

"Lance doesn't want me anymore," I whisper. He could have picked a more mature way of breaking up with me than getting a blow job from another man. In public, no less. But then again, I could have picked a more mature way to precipitate our breakup than getting a series of piercings I knew he wouldn't find appealing.

"I wanted to decorate myself," I say. "For you."

Logan rewards me by closing his hands together and giving me a long, firm stroke from root to tip. "For who?" His voice is a low growl and holy shit, I might come again before we get much farther.

"For you. *Daddy*," I say, and I absolutely cannot keep myself from arching my back and thrusting into his hands.

"Oh, my baby boy," he says, and there's something about the tenderness in his voice and the absolute filthiness of him calling me that while stroking my dick that makes my head swim and my heart ache.

Four

LOGAN

I'LL NEVER UNDERSTAND how Lance could be so fucking stupid. Getting a clandestine blow job at a party was bad enough. Doing it at my law firm's holiday party was a reckless, asshole move that I'm still supremely pissed at him about.

But betraying his boyfriend—the guy he's been dating for two years—who he asked to move in with him when they finished college...I just can't fathom how I've raised a son who can hurt someone the way he's hurt Silas.

I suppose I'm looking for a little revenge here, too. Fucking my son's ex-boyfriend—especially so soon after Lance's betrayal—is surely a terrible idea. Which is precisely why I didn't take advantage of him in the taxi. He was drunk and angry and the hottest thing I've seen in a long time.

I should be the grownup who makes the same sensible decision tonight.

But I'm not a saint and there's only so much resistance I can put up, especially with him here, naked, sober, and so very willing. On his back like this, his legs spread, the piercings lining his cock shiny with the fluid he's leaking.

Still, there's a power differential between us and I'd have to be a monster not to be aware of it. There's the difference in our ages, for one thing. And in our social and economic status.

I have a highly successful career and a comfortable lifestyle. Silas graduated from college less than a year ago and has been living with my son in a condo bought with Lance's trust fund.

I'm not worried about my reputation, exactly. Silas is young enough to be my son, yes, but he is an adult. Most people in my professional life know I'm gay. I'm the partner liaison to my firm's LGBTQ affinity group. I don't bring dates to firm functions, but that's because I don't have serious relationships. The twinks I hook up with on Grindr are always one night only.

Silas is exactly my type—young, slim, and pretty, with a generous mouth that's currently red-bitten and wet from his tongue licking his lips. The multiple piercings are the icing on the cake. My mouth is already watering at the thought of sucking that long, beautifully decorated cock.

His hands are clenching and unclenching at his sides and his cock is dripping with precome. I've spent the last couple of years suppressing my attraction to Silas and I never expected to have him. There's nothing I'll deny him now. If he's willing, I'll have him every way I can think of until he's ready to move on.

I put all thoughts of my inconsiderate son aside and focus on Silas. "You're so gorgeous, baby boy," I tell him. I adjust my erection under my lounge pants and Silas's eyes go to my crotch.

"I'm feeling a little underdressed here," he says. His hand drifts down to his cock and idly toys with the barbells of his ladder piercing. He's hairless around his cock and balls, clean and smooth everywhere, and his flat stomach quivers as he plays with himself. "I want to see you, too," he says, a little shyly. It's a tantalizing combination, that hint of shyness while he's spread out naked on my sofa, touching himself and looking at me with flushed cheeks and a puffy, pouting mouth.

"Soon," I promise.

I take Silas's hand off his cock and push both arms over his head. They dangle over the arm of the sofa, which makes his chest arch and his nipples bud tall and proud. I'll make him come playing with them again later, but I want his cock and I want it now.

I give his cock a long, firm stroke from root to tip, and then I wrap my fingers around the base, tilt it to the angle I want, and bend my head to finally get my mouth on it.

Silas's hips jerk up as soon as my lips touch the head of his dick and I press my other hand down on his hip. "Do I need to tie you down to keep you still?"

"Sorry, Daddy." He's panting heavily and I will most certainly be tying him down later, just for the pleasure of watching his lithe, young body squirm in my restraints. "I'll be good."

"Can you?" Because I'm hovering just above his cock and his hips are still making tiny thrusts up, trying to meet his dick with my lips. I'm not sure he even knows he's doing it.

A bead of fluid wells up around the pearl protruding from his slit. I lick it from his tip and Silas moans. His stomach is quivering, his thighs are shaking, and his hands are clenched around the arm of the sofa behind his head. "Please," he whimpers. "Please, Daddy. Please suck me."

"That's my good boy," I praise him. "Ask for what you want and Daddy will give it to you."

I dip my head and take Silas's cock into my mouth. Silas groans loud and long and I think he's going to come immediately, but he holds himself back somehow. I stay still for a moment, loving the weight of him filling my mouth, getting used to the feel of his piercings on my tongue. The pearl at the tip nudges the back of my throat.

I peer up Silas's body and he's staring down at me sucking him. "God, that's so hot," he whispers.

I hollow my cheeks and suck as I slowly draw up his length. I'm extra careful with my teeth and the bump of each barbell as my bottom lip passes over them makes Silas jolt every time.

He's looking down at me and I keep looking at him. Up the length of his body, his quivering stomach, his heaving chest. He's beautiful, this boy, and I'm torn between making him come as fast as I can and torturing him with how long and slow I can make it.

I settle on a steady sucking rhythm, swirling my tongue around the beads in his slit and under the head of his cock, then a side-to-side sweeping lick at each barbell in the ladder. I take more each time I suck him down, until my nose is pressed against the smooth bare skin at the base and the head of his cock is in my throat.

That's when he comes, with me swallowing around him. His cock jerks in my mouth, but his hips do not, even if every muscle in his legs and torso is strained to the breaking point with the effort to keep still.

To obey, like the good boy I asked him to be.

I let him ride out his orgasm, holding him in my mouth until he stops quivering and starts to soften. Then I kneel up, and pull my cock out of my pants. It's thicker than Silas's and probably shorter, and Silas lurches up and scrambles around so that he's on his hands and knees, his mouth already open and drooling for my cock.

"That's it, boy." I grab him by the hair at the back of his head and stuff my cock into his mouth. "Take your Daddy's cock like a good boy."

I don't give him time to adjust, just thrust as deep as I can into his mouth, and tighten my fingers in his hair. His eyes roll to the back of his head, then slip closed, and for Christ's sake, I knew—just *knew*—that he would be perfect.

His full lips are clamped around my cock and his tongue is soft, his jaw relaxed. I set up a punishing rhythm of thrusts, fucking his face as hard as I dare. Tears start slipping down his cheeks, but he makes no move to get away or stop me. His mouth is wet and hot and I can feel the give at the back of his throat.

"Fuck, boy, do you even have a gag reflex?"

His eyebrows twitch upwards and he blinks his tear-filled eyes open, looking up at me. He can't speak because my cock is halfway down his throat, or shake his head because I'm holding it immobile with my hand tangled tight in his hair, but his eyes shine up at me with no small amount of pride.

I come with a roar down his throat, pulling his head against me and grinding his nose into my pubic bone.

Five

SILAS

MY BRAIN PANICS when Logan floods my throat with a rush of hot, thick come. I can't swallow fast enough and it drips down my chin, along with the tears streaming from my eyes. But I know how to do this, even if Logan's cock is thicker than Lance's, bigger than any I've sucked before. I stay still, letting Logan support my head, keeping my jaw and throat open.

It's really only a second or two that I can't breathe because my nose is mashed against his groin. He's not shaved down there, like me, but the hairs are trimmed short and barely tickle the inside of my nose.

Just when my brain is screaming at me to struggle to get away, to breathe again, Logan loosens his grip on the back of my neck and slides his hand around to cup my chin. He draws his softening cock from my throat way more gently than he'd thrust into it and cradles my face in his big hands while I suck in several huge breaths of glorious oxygen.

He tilts my face up to his. Shit, I must look an absolute mess. Tears and snot and come are smeared all over my cheeks and chin. My lips are probably swollen and red, my eyes no doubt red-rimmed, and I bet my eyeliner has melted into raccoon rings. Logan looks at me like he's never seen anything like me.

He sits back on his heels, then lets go of me long enough to tuck his dick back in his pants and pull his T-shirt off over his head. He swings his legs around so he's sitting properly on the sofa and beckons me closer with a finger. "Come here, baby boy. Let Daddy clean you up."

I crawl closer, still on my hands and knees, and he wipes my face with his T-shirt. The fabric is soft on my abused lips and gummy eyelashes and he scrubs gently at the tracks on my cheeks. Then he gathers me into his lap. I fold my knees and curl my spine into him and he wraps his arms around me. I'm too tall for this, really, but it's so...*nice*...being cuddled like this.

Lance usually just rolls over and falls asleep when we're done.

"Look," he murmurs into my ear and his finger points at our reflections in the fireplace glass. "We look good together, don't you think?"

I look. At me, Silas Mitchell, bare-assed naked, bent and tucked into the body of my ex-boyfriend's father. My head is resting on his shoulder and his arms are locked around me. The bronze tan of his forearms contrasts with the paleness of my side and hip. His head is bent to mine and the salt and pepper of his close beard is nearly hidden behind my blond hair. He kisses the top of my head three or four times, then leans it back against the sofa.

I can't pull my eyes away from the image. He looks...peaceful. More so than when I first arrived, when he had a lingering furrow between his eyebrows and his eyes looked tired, like he'd been working on his laptop for too many hours in a row. He also doesn't look guilty or ashamed of what we just did. He's just holding me in his arms.

And I...I look relaxed. There's no tension in my muscles. I don't feel like my shoulders are hunched around my ears like I've been feeling for the last week. My face is still blotchy and my lips still puffy, but I look well-fucked and pleased about it.

"Yeah," I finally say, even though Logan hasn't demanded an answer. "We do."

Logan lifts his head and tucks a knuckle under my chin, tipping my face up to his. He kisses me on the lips and my stomach drops away. Just a sweet, gentle closed-mouth kiss at first. Then another, and another, and then I can't take it anymore and I part my lips, hoping for more.

He parts his too, and the tip of his tongue traces delicately just inside my lips. It flicks into my mouth, glancing against my tongue, then retreats, and I follow. He's moved his hand from my chin to my jaw, holding me gently and rubbing his thumb on my cheekbone while he kisses me softly and sweetly. Like I'm too delicate for rough treatment, even though he literally just fucked my throat so hard I feel like I swallowed gravel.

I don't know how to feel about this. I came here for a quick revenge fuck. Well, I'd kind of hoped it wouldn't be *too* quick. But I hadn't expected this level of cuddling and care, and it's doing something weird to my chest and stomach.

To avoid thinking about it—always best to avoid thinking too much about the dudes you fuck, or at least that seems to be Lance's mantra—I take control of the kiss and deepen it. I swing my legs around so I'm straddling Logan and thrust my tongue into his mouth. He responds in kind and we're sucking at each other's tongues. I can taste my come on his tongue and he can surely taste his on mine.

It's wet and sloppy and super hot. His scruff rubs against my abused mouth and the slight burn would make my dick wake up and take notice if it hadn't just been sucked dry.

But all the while, his hands are gently stroking me. Not gripping my neck or pulling my hair like he did while I was sucking him off. No, he's combing his fingers through my hair and stroking my forehead and temples and tracing around the shell of my ears and I feel like I'm about to cry or something, which is really dumb, so I pull back to catch my breath.

The last thing I want Logan to think is that I'm a needy, emotional kid, so I bend my head so he can't see how close to tears I am. I've got one hand braced against his chest and I focus on that to give myself time to recover.

His chest is broad and his pecs are firm under a mat of salt and pepper hair. I run my hand through the fluff of it and my fingers glance across the hard bud of a nipple. I rub at it and pinch it gently between my fingers. It doesn't seem like his nipples are nearly as sensitive as mine, but it hardens a little more and Logan says softly, "That's nice, Silas."

I give his other nipple the same treatment. Logan sweeps his hands up and down my back. His dick is slowly swelling beneath me and mine is plumping up again too. It's not the urgent need to touch and suck and fuck we were gripped in earlier. It's more like a slow build of anticipation and uncurling desire.

It has the effect I'd hoped of distracting me from my feelings, but before it gets to a point where either of us does anything about it, Logan stills my hands on his chest. "Let's clean up and go to bed, baby boy."

I take in a deep breath and nod. Right, yeah. I've agreed to stay the weekend.

It's gonna be weird to stay in this house that I'm so familiar with but without Lance. I know where Logan's bedroom is—on the second floor, at the back of the house—but I've never been inside it. What reason would I have had, to be in the bedroom of my boyfriend's dad?

I could back out, if I wanted to. Say I've gotten the revenge I wanted and thanks for the two orgasms and the snuggle, but I'd better get back to the city. Except that I still haven't sorted out where I'm going to live, now that Lance and I are broken up. I've been crashing on an air mattress in Chloe's apartment, but that's temporary, not least because she's got three roommates. They've been cool about it, but I really gotta figure out what the hell I'm going to do.

Speaking of Chloe, there's a muted buzz somewhere on the floor from my phone. Shit, I told her I was going out tonight to find someone to fuck and she's checking in with me to make sure I'm okay. I do that for her when she goes out.

I didn't tell her that it was Logan I was planning to fuck.

My phone buzzes again, and again. Logan lifts me off his lap with as much ease as if I were actually a little boy and digs through my clothes strewn around the floor until he finds my phone, then hands it to me. "Text your friend, baby, and tell them you're safe. I'm going to clean up and turn the kitchen lights out. Come upstairs when you're ready."

I open Chloe's message.

you okay, dude?

Chloe doesn't bother with capitalization in texts.

when are you coming home?

Chloe's apartment isn't my home—I don't have a home any-more—but I love her for welcoming me into hers.

Staying out.

I tap back with my thumbs.

Three dots appear while she's tapping out her reply, then disappear, then reappear. I give her a minute, because she knows that Lance is the only guy I've slept with after sex. Fucking or sucking cock is one thing, but actually sleeping together is way more intimate.

While I'm waiting for her reply, I should pick up my clothes that are strewn all around the living room, but before I can haul my ass off the sofa, Logan's back from the kitchen and already doing it.

are you sure? i'm all for a good rebound fuck, but is staying the night with a stranger a good idea?

Logan is anything but a stranger, but Chloe doesn't know that. There's another three dots, but I reply before she sends her next message.

> I'm fine.

I type back.

> He's not a stranger. He's...

I glance at Logan, currently folding my jeans over his arm, and picking up my mesh shirt, his come-covered T-shirt, and my socks and underwear. He catches my eye, jerks a thumb in the direction of the stairs to the lower level, and mouths *laundry* at me. I nod and look back at my phone.

He's what? A friend? Family? Shit, I don't know what Logan is to me now. And I'm suddenly too tired to think about it anymore.

> It's complicated.

I text Chloe.

> But I'm safe, I swear.

> I'll call you tomorrow.

> you better.

> or i'm tracking your location and coming to get you.

I send a heart emoji to her and she sends one back to me. I turn my phone screen off and find Logan in the laundry room downstairs.

He's got the washer started and is standing in front of it, one hand on the closed lid and the other threaded through his hair. He looks lost in thought and I wonder if he regrets asking me to stay.

But then he turns and sees me hovering in the doorway, and he smiles wide enough that his eyes crinkle at the corners.

"Shower first, then bed." His voice is firm, but I know I can refuse. I can leave if I want, or crash on the sofa, or hell, he'd probably let me stay over in Lance's room, if I asked.

Logan would never force me to do anything I don't want to do. I know that with a hundred percent certainty. But he comes to me, puts his hands on my shoulders, and turns me so that I'm facing out of the laundry room. Toward the stairs to the main level and the next set of stairs to the top floor. To his bedroom.

He gives a gentle push at the middle of my back and my feet start moving. I don't have to make a decision. All I need to do right now is what Logan tells me to do. And that feels as good as the mind-blowing orgasms he's given me.

Six

LOGAN

SILAS'S SHOULDERS ARE relaxed when he walks naked up the stairs in front of me. Not like they were when he arrived at my house earlier this evening. Then, his shoulders were turned inward and hunched up toward his ears. It could have been the cold—I got the sense he was hanging out on the porch for a while.

Gathering his courage to knock on my door, probably. It took a lot of guts for him to proposition me. The kind of guts fueled by white-hot anger and betrayal, sure, but not the kind of guts I'd've had. No matter how attractive I found Silas, I would never have made the first move on him.

He's too young for me. He was my son's boyfriend for two years. He wasn't even old enough to drink when I met him. His slim hips sway a little and the globes of his buttocks clench and release as he climbs the stairs before me.

I want him so much. Not just for the weekend. I put the kibosh on that thought immediately, though. He's not mine. He's pissed at Lance and probably grieving the life he thought they were going to have, and he's here for a rebound fuck, with the added benefit of revenge.

I can give him that, even though I shouldn't. But what I can't have is this precious boy as my own, permanently. He'll get over Lance. I love my son, but Silas deserves better.

And then Silas will find someone his own age. Someone who appreciates him for who he is, piercings and all.

In the meantime, though, I've got him for tonight. I steer him to my bedroom and march him straight to the ensuite bathroom. "Stay there," I tell him and he stands obediently in the middle of the large room while I strip my lounge pants and underwear off.

He looks me up and down with heavily-lidded eyes and my cock stirs. I've got a personal trainer who keeps me in shape and I swim several times a week, but I'm not in my twenties anymore and the years have definitely taken their toll.

Silas doesn't look like he minds too much. His tongue darts out and licks his lips while his eyes are locked on my cock. But he's also swaying on his feet a little and needs to be cleaned up and get some sleep. I wonder how much sleep he's been getting since Lance betrayed him.

I turn away from him and get the shower running. It's a double wide standalone shower with the biggest rainfall shower head my designer could find when I had the house renovated. There's a detachable shower head and a line of jets on the side wall. It's luxurious and decadent and it cost a goddamn fortune to put in, but my designer was right that it would be worth every penny. It's pretty much my favorite place in the house. Well, second to the giant soaking tub that's on the other end of the bathroom.

I like a nice bubble bath as much as a long, hot shower—so sue me.

I adjust the temperature and motion to Silas. "Get in, baby."

He drifts toward me, his bare feet whispering on the marble tiled floor, and I hold his elbow as he steps over the short ledge and into the shower. His eyes close immediately and his head tilts back under the spray.

There's room for both of us under it, but I still crowd as close as I can to him. I run my hands over his silken, wet skin. He sighs and drapes his arms around my neck.

"That's it, baby boy," I croon in his ear. "Let Daddy clean you up and then we'll go to bed."

He nods and rests his head on my shoulder. I grab the soap and rub it briskly between my hands, working up a cedar- and pine-scented lather. I soap up his back and shoulders first, then as much of his arms as I can reach while they're still draped over my shoulders, then I rub my soapy hands over his ass. I slide my fingers in between his cheeks and rub his hole until he's squirming against me and his hardening cock pokes against my stomach.

"Have to get you all clean for me," I whisper and he shivers. "Tomorrow, though."

He whines when I pull my fingers away, but I turn him around and prop his back against my chest. His dick juts out and curves upward, and mine nestles between his ass cheeks. I soap his chest and neck first and he arches into my hands when my palms graze over his nipples.

He's breathing hard and his head is lolling against my shoulder. He's utterly pliant, though, letting me position his body and move his limbs where I want him. "Such a good boy, Silas," I praise him.

I soap his cock last, lathering it thoroughly, squeezing and stroking until he comes with a soft moan, striping the shower wall. He's a rag doll in my arms now and I'll take him to bed in just a moment.

But first, I let him sink down and sit cross-legged on the tiled floor, leaning against the shower wall, while I wash myself with hurried efficiency. He's watching me and his mouth is slightly open, and when I soap my own aching hard cock, I can't resist.

It takes only a few strokes and I come, too, all over his upturned face.

He smiles sleepily and licks what he can reach with his tongue. I clean the rest of my come from his face with a washcloth, then turn the shower off, and tug him gently out onto the fluffy bath mat. I grab a towel and dry him off, then dry myself off as quickly as I can.

I brush my teeth, find a new toothbrush for Silas and tell him to use it, then steer this sweet, sleepy boy to my bedroom. I pull back the covers and nestle him in the bed, then get in next to him, and pull the covers over us.

He immediately curls into me and I cuddle him close, his head on my shoulder and my arm around his. I expect him to fall asleep immediately, but his hand is resting on my chest and he starts...well, petting me, for lack of a better word.

He strokes me from collarbone to navel and runs his fingers through my chest hair. "Logan?" He keeps petting me and I'm about to fall asleep myself any minute.

"Mmmm?"

"Thanks."

"For what?" I feel his shoulders shrug under my arm, but his hand is still petting, and his fingers trace the occasional swirl over my skin. It's been ages since I've let a hookup stay the night and I've forgotten how nice it is to be touched with such sweetness.

"For...you know, the sex and whatever." His voice is soft. "For not turning me away. For taking care of me."

I tighten my arm around him, drawing him closer, and kiss the top of his head. "I will never turn you away, Silas. And I'll take care of you as long as you want."

Forever, is what I mean. But it's far too soon to even think about that. I don't want to scare the boy, so I just kiss the top of his head again. "Now, go to sleep."

He turns his head slightly and presses a soft kiss to my nipple. "Yes, Daddy."

I fall asleep with him in my arms as if he were really my boy.

Seven

SILAS

I WAKE SLOWLY and little things gradually worm into my consciousness. A warm, hard body pressed against my back. Hot breath puffing against my ear and open-mouthed kisses at the nape of my neck. A hard cock nestled between my ass cheeks.

"You awake?" Logan's arm snakes over me to pinch a nipple.

"I am now." I squirm against his cock and I can feel it swelling even more. "Are you going to fuck me?"

Logan keeps playing with my nipples and my own morning wood is harder than it's ever been.

"Have you done anal before?" Unspoken between us is the question *With Lance?* and it's a good thing he's behind me and can't see my face.

I turn and bury it in the pillow anyway, for good measure, and my voice is muffled when I say, "Yeah, loads of times."

Logan's hand stills and his hips pull away so that his cock is no longer touching me. I squirm back to get close to him again, but he moves far enough away to turn me onto my back. He catches my chin in a firm grip and turns my face to his.

"Really?" His hair is mussed and there's a pillow crease across his cheek. He's the sexiest man I've ever seen and he's looking at me with fatherly concern and fucking hell, the combination is so dirty and *wrong*. I can't believe how hot it is.

"Silas." It's a warning if ever I've heard one and I can bull-shit my way through a lot of things, but I don't think I can lie to Logan. Or, I could try, but I'm pretty sure he'd know and then he'd be disappointed in me. And my heart turns over in this weird way at the thought of disappointing him.

"No," I confess.

"Jesus, what did you and Lance do together?" The question kind of bursts out of him and he looks a little pissed, but I don't think it's at me. He closes his eyes for a second and slides his hand from my chin up my jaw, cradling my face. "I'm sorry, I shouldn't have asked that. It's none of my business."

I shrug. "Mostly blow jobs and hand jobs." I don't know why I'm telling him this. It feels like a betrayal of Lance, telling his dad that our sex life didn't satisfy me.

But then I remember that Lance actually betrayed *me* and that's why I'm here, in his dad's bed. I still haven't gotten the revenge fuck I came here for and the vision in my head of me impaled on Logan's cock makes my hole clench in desperate anticipation.

"Lance thought it was gross and never wanted to try it."

Logan shakes his head. "He's an idiot."

I completely agree. But Logan doesn't turn me onto my stomach and fuck me like I want. Instead, he smoothes my hair back from my forehead and bends to kiss my neck. He nudges his head under my ear and presses a line of open-mouthed kisses from my ear to the hollow between my collarbones. He fastens his mouth over one nipple and sucks hard, making me arch my chest into him, and plays with the other, tugging and twisting the ring until I'm panting and wriggling under him.

He switches mouth and fingers on my nipples and I am a freaking mess. I'm tossing my head on the pillow and jerking my hips up, seeking friction on my cock. He rolls on top of me to give it to me. My legs spread wide, then I wrap them about his hips, hooking my ankles together at his lower back.

Our cocks are lined up and his hips rock against mine. The slow slide of our dicks together, sandwiched between our bodies, drives me crazy. The rings piercing the underside of my dick shift each time his hips rock against me. Logan is still sucking and playing with my nipples and I'm going to come any second now. I whine out his name. "Logan, please."

He stops everything. Stops rocking his hips, stops sucking and biting at my right nipple, stops twisting my left with his fingers. I tighten my legs around him to get him to keep going, but he's an unmovable weight pressing me down.

I'm in agony.

He braces himself on his elbows and looks down at me. "What did you say?" The laugh lines on his face and the silver in his hair remind me.

"Daddy. Please. Fuck me. I want you inside me."

"You'll get me, baby boy," he promises, but he doesn't change position to do it. Asshole. "But you've never done it before and we need to take it slow."

"I've fingered myself before." I reach a hand down toward my ass, like I'm about to show him. "I can get three fingers in. I can take it."

Logan grabs my wrist and pulls my arm over my head. Then he does the same to my other arm and holds both my wrists in one hand. It shifts his weight so more of him comes down on my cock. The mat of hair covering his stomach rubs deliciously over my aching shaft with each breath he takes.

He squeezes my wrists in his big hand and looks sternly into my eyes. "We'll do it my way or we won't do it at all. Is that clear, Silas?"

I give in, because what else am I going to do? And also because something turns over in my stomach when he goes all commanding like that. I nod. "Yes, Daddy."

"That's my good boy," he says. He lets go of my wrists.

I keep my arms over my head and clasp my wrists to keep that sensation of being held down. I'm stretched out beneath him, triangulated with his mouth and hands on my nipples, and his hips pressing down on my cock. I come like that in two seconds, arching my back to rub my dick against his.

He keeps his motions up while I shiver and jerk beneath him. When my orgasm finally stops crashing over me and the aftershocks fade, I'm a loose, sprawling mess. My legs drop away from his hips and my hands unclench around my wrists.

Logan gives both nipples a last, sweet kiss each, then levers himself up to his knees. He swipes his hand through the come striping my belly and starts jacking his cock.

He's looking at me while he does it and the intensity in his gaze pins me. "Such a beautiful boy," he says. His hand moves faster. "You're my beautiful boy." His face is flushed with arousal, his fingers white with my come slicking his cock, but his eyes are still boring into mine. Like he knows what he's saying, even through the heat of his lust.

"Mine," he growls, and that word digs deep into my chest, hooking claws into my heart that I try to ignore. He can't mean it, not really. He's just saying the kind of things that you say in the heat of the moment. He comes all over me, marking me with white ropes of his come, mixing with my own already painting my chest and stomach.

He rests his ass on his heels and his heavy breathing slowly calms. When he looks at me, the hard expression he had while jerking himself off eases, and his eyes go soft. He leans forward, hovering over me, and kisses my cheek, then smooths the hair back from my forehead. "Sleep a while longer, if you want, Silas."

So I do, because why not? It's not like I had any particular plans for today. I've been so focused on Lance and his betrayal, then on getting here and seducing his dad, that I haven't really planned any farther than that. I still need to figure out where I'm going to live, but I don't have the energy to think about that now.

Or about whether Logan meant it when he said I was his.

I'm not sure how long I doze, but at some point, Logan comes back to the bed. His hair is wet and he smells of soap and citrus shampoo. He's dressed in gray slacks and a white Oxford shirt under a rich chocolate brown sweater that makes his hazel eyes bright.

"Rise and shine, baby boy," he coaxes and I stretch beneath the covers.

"Why are you dressed?" I ask. "I thought we were going to spend the day in bed."

He draws back when I reach toward him, and grabs my hand to pull me up. "Up," he says.

He's brought my clothes from last night upstairs. He lays my jeans on the end of the bed and puts a folded long-sleeve shirt from his own dresser on top. Clean boxers and socks, also from his dresser. He puts the rest of my clothes from last night in a tidy pile on the edge of the dresser.

"Why?" I pull my knees up to my chest under the covers, fold my arms over my knees, and rest my chin on them. "Wouldn't you rather come back to bed and fuck me properly?"

He gives me a look. "Silas. Don't make me tell you again."

I drop my eyes and study the navy blue diamond pattern on the quilt covering the bed. "Yes, Daddy."

He leaves the room and I hear his tread heading downstairs.

I wander into the bathroom, take a piss, and get in the shower. I was so sleepy and sex-sated last night that I hardly remember last night's shower with him. Damn, his shower is amazing.

The rainfall shower head beats down on my shoulders and the side jets make short work of the come smeared over my chest and stomach. I wash my hair with Logan's citrusy shampoo and take my time enjoying his shower.

It feels pretty inappropriate to be in Lance's dad's shower. Even though we sucked each other off last night and both came this morning with Logan rubbing all over me, standing in his shower, surrounded by the products that make Logan smell the way he does, and touching myself feels super dirty.

Especially when I soap between my ass cheeks and press the tip of my finger against my hole. I turn my back to one of the side jets and bend over a little, spreading my cheeks so the spray washes the soap away. It takes a little experimentation, but eventually I find a position bent over and spread enough that a jet of water aims right at my hole.

Oh shit, that's good. I take my dick in one hand and keep the other spreading my ass open as much as I can. There's a short knock at the door that I left half-open and Logan pokes his head in. I start and look at him guiltily. He didn't say I couldn't jerk off in the shower, but it's a natural reaction when someone finds you with your dick in your hand about to shoot, you know?

Logan raises an eyebrow. "I suspected as much," he says. "You're really desperate for something to fill that hole, aren't you, boy?"

I go hot and I'm sure I'm blushing bright red, but I'm close enough to orgasm that I don't care. "Want it to be you, Daddy," I manage to say around a moan.

Logan doesn't come any farther into the bathroom, but through the steam fogging the glass of the shower door, I can see a bulge filling the front of his slacks. He leans against the doorway and crosses one leg over his ankle. He's dressed like it's casual Friday at his firm and I'm naked, in his shower, bent over, ass spread to the jets of water, my cock filling my hand.

"Your breakfast is getting cold," Logan says and the stern expression on his face only makes me hotter. "But, by all means, if this is how you'd rather spend your time..."

He's going to just stand there and watch, isn't he? I squirm a little closer to the jet of water pounding my hole and speed up the hand jacking my dick. Logan's face is impassive, his mouth tipped down at the corners in a little frown. The only way I can tell he's affected by me at all is that bulge in his pants, which is bigger now. He's not touching himself, though.

He's just staring at me with that little frown and those stern eyes and I feel like a naughty schoolboy caught by the headmaster. It is so freaking hot.

I'm furiously stripping my dick and wiggling my ass in the water spray and my eyes are rolling back into my head. And then a movement from Logan catches my eye and I see him ease the cuff of one sleeve back. He glances at his watch and looks back at me.

"Any time now," he says and I don't know, maybe it's the complete indifference in his voice that tips me over the edge.

"Ahhh," I moan as I come as hard as I came this morning. It makes my knees weak and I slap the hand that was gripping my ass against the shower wall to keep myself from falling over. I duck my head under the shower spray and let the water pound on the back of my neck. My wet hair is hanging in my face and I'm panting through the aftershocks. Whoa. That was intense.

By the time I look up at the bathroom doorway again, it's empty.

Eight

LOGAN

MY LEGS ARE RUBBERY AND MY COCK IS SO HARD, it's difficult to walk. I brace one hand on the dresser in my bedroom and palm myself through my slacks. I want to turn around, go back to the bathroom, bend Silas facedown over the sink counter, and shove my cock into him.

He'd be willing, I know. And so tight. The vision of his narrow back and hips writhing when he's speared on my cock is blinding. Until I see my hand on the dresser surface, imagine it pressed on the back of Silas's neck, and catch a glimpse of my face in the mirror.

My face is flushed a dark red, and my pupils have swallowed the hazel of my irises. There's a hard set to my lips and I look...mean, for lack of a better word.

Cruel.

Ready to hurt him for my own pleasure.

I squeeze my cock hard enough that it pulses in my hand.

I won't do that.

Not yet, anyway. Silas might like a bit of pain with his pleasure—the multiple piercings in the most sensitive areas of his body strongly suggest that. But he's never been fucked in the ass before and I am not such a monster as to pound into him with no prep.

Even if I am the monster who plans to fuck the virgin ass of my son's ex-boyfriend.

Back to my original plan. Breakfast, then the delivery I've arranged. I've got a few toys we could use, but Silas isn't just a random hookup. I placed the order already and chose items to use specifically for him, and only him.

God bless the internet, where you can not only order sex toys, but hire someone to pick them up for you.

I resolutely turn my thoughts away from the beautiful naked boy in my shower and what I plan to do to him later. A minute or two later, my erection starts to fade and I hear the shower turn off.

By the time Silas comes downstairs, I'm on my second cup of coffee. "Eat," I say, pointing at the plate of eggs and bacon I'd set on the island countertop in front of the chair next to me. The food is cold, but that's the consequence of taking too long in his shower this morning.

I pour him a fresh cup of coffee, though, and add the amount of cream and sugar I know he likes. He looks surprised, but he and Lance have spent enough time in my house that I've had plenty of opportunities to observe what he likes and dislikes.

In fact, Lance and I used to make breakfast together for Silas on Saturday mornings when they stayed over here. Cooking together is a ritual that dates back to when Lance was growing up and we continued it on any weekends the boys stayed over. We've tried all the traditional breakfast foods—eggs every way we could think of, sausage or bacon we'd buy at the farmer's market, pancakes or French toast, hash browns or home fries —and a slew of more elaborate dishes too. Huevos rancheros, eggs Benedict, a variety of quiches and omelettes.

I like cooking and I like spending time with my kid, even if he's been a disappointing asshole to his boyfriend.

Silas usually slept later than Lance and would wander into the kitchen, sleep-creased and hair sticking up every which way. Lance would mock him for doctoring his coffee and not drinking it black the way he and I prefer, and Silas would scarf down the food we made with gratifying and messy enthusiasm.

When I'm alone, breakfast is less elaborate, but I've ordered groceries to be delivered as well, to cook Silas dinner tonight.

Silas forks up some eggs and chomps a slice of bacon in half. His eyes are darting from his plate to me, sidelong from under the fall of his hair.

Yeah, it's a little strange to me, too. Having breakfast in this kitchen together, but without Lance. Especially after what we did last night. And this morning.

"How's your musical coming along?" I ask him. Silas's senior theater project—a queer retelling of the Oedipus myth as a contemporary space opera—had a limited run as a student-led production last spring, but I know he hopes to someday see it performed on Broadway.

"Ugh, still revising it," he says. "There were some things that didn't work the way I'd expected in the first production, so I'm trying to figure out how to change them."

"That's normal, right?" I know a number of Broadway and off-Broadway producers and playwrights. Mostly through work, though I typically represent the producers and less frequently the creatives, but I'm also a dyed-in-the-wool theater buff. It's why I got into entertainment law in the first place.

I keep an eye on the emerging and avant-garde stuff, too. Last year, for Silas's birthday, I took the boys to a production of Euripides' *The Bacchae* in Harlem that Lance called deeply fucked up. He wasn't entirely wrong about that, but Silas and I loved it.

I suspected it was part of the inspiration for his musical, but now I'm wondering if that came from somewhere else.

"It's a little on the nose, isn't it?"

He stuffs the other half piece of bacon in his mouth and asks around it, "What is?"

"Choosing Oedipus and making him queer. It's almost like you have daddy issues or something."

I wink at him to show that I'm not kink-shaming him, but I'm genuinely curious. "How did you come up with the idea?"

I think I'm actually asking when he came up with the idea. As in, before or after Lance first brought him to meet me? Before or after he realized he was attracted to me?

I suppose it's not really important. I've met enough writers who are completely normal, yet pen the wildest, weirdest stuff, that I know the imagination is limitless. Not everything a person writes is necessarily autobiographical.

Silas shrugs. "I read the original play in high school. I mean, obviously not the original ancient Greek, but one of those dry translations that was required in my AP English class."

I dimly remember those days. I don't think my high school English classes required *Oedipus Rex*, but I recall we read *Antigone* and *The Odyssey* and Euripides' *Medea*. Can't say that I was ever inspired to rewrite any of those stories. But then again, I'm not a playwright and Silas is.

"The original story is so dumb, you know?" Silas is saying. "I mean, it's all because of this prophecy that Oedipus's parents receive when he's born. That he'll grow up to kill his father. So, naturally, his father orders his mother to kill him." Silas rolls his eyes and I chuckle. "But she can't, because you know, she's not a monster."

"Monster enough to give the baby to a servant to kill, if I recall correctly," I say.

"Fair point," Silas agrees. "But the servant doesn't kill baby Oedipus and instead gives him to a shepherd, who gives him to the king of Corinth who doesn't have any kids of his own. Anyway, my whole point is that if Oedipus's parents had ignored the stupid prophecy, Oedipus would have grown up knowing who his parents were. Probably would've become king after his father died of old age or whatever. Definitely wouldn't have fucked his mother."

"In your version, he fucks his father," I observe. The whole concept sounds ludicrous, but I saw his student production and it actually works. Somehow, Silas managed to bring the classic Greek tragedy to life in a way that was both innovative and entertaining.

"Yeah," Silas says with a cheeky grin.

Which brings us back to my original question. "And you want to fuck your almost father-in-law."

"Yeah," Silas says, only this time, there's a shadow of uncertainty on his face. Then it clears a little. "Oh, is this a life-imitating-art kind of thing? Is that what you're asking?"

"Or art imitating life?"

Silas looks thoughtful for a moment, then shrugs. "I dunno. Does it matter?"

It shouldn't, I suppose. What difference does it make if Silas wrote his play before or after he realized he was attracted to me? It isn't as if the order of operations makes what we've been doing—or will do—together any less complicated.

He still came here to get revenge on his cheating ex. My son.

And I'm going along with it. I haven't fucked his virgin ass —yet—but I've lost track of how many times I've made him come and he's been here less than twenty-four hours.

Silas pushes the rest of his eggs around his plate with his last piece of bacon. "Do you not want me to call you Daddy anymore?"

He's trying to sound nonchalant, I can tell, and I kick myself for making him doubt how much I want that. How much I want him.

I reach out and put my hand over his. "I do want that, Silas. You were right last night that I've wanted to do all kinds of things with you, even when you were with Lance."

I've never let myself fantasize about them—much—because it was never going to happen. Until now.

"But I don't want you to call me that unless it's what you want, too. Don't do it just because you think it's what I want."

It's been a long time since I was in the kink scene. It's easy enough to find a young man on Grindr who likes it a bit rough or who doesn't mind a spanking when I'm in the mood for that. But I've never asked a hookup to call me Daddy. And I've never had someone I wanted to call my boy. It's a lifestyle I haven't made the time to pursue.

Until Silas said the word and made me wonder what I've been missing.

Silas looks at me and his green eyes are serious under his blond brows. "I have a dad, you know. He's an accountant in Maryland. He's boring as fuck—spends all his free time going on bird-watching trips—but he's a nice guy. Never spanked me when I was growing up, didn't make me feel bad about myself when I screwed up. He doesn't really get me, you know? He doesn't understand why I want to live in New York City, much less wait tables and write weird plays that may never get produced, when I could do something practical like accounting or whatever."

He blinks and smiles a little. "But he loves me, you know? And I love him. Like a real dad, okay? I don't want to fuck him." He shudders and makes a grimace that conveys his disgust at the idea. "So I don't have 'daddy issues,' all right? I just like calling you Daddy. It's hot and I know it's kind of dirty and wrong because you were almost kind of my father-in-law, but it's the good kind of dirty and wrong."

He slips off his stool and I swivel sideways on mine so he can slide in between my legs. He slides his hands up my thighs toward my groin and we both watch my cock slowly tent the fly of my slacks.

"Isn't it?" He looks up at me with wide eyes.

"Yeah, baby," I say. "It is."

Silas sighs and his eyes dip closed. "I like that, too. When you call me 'baby' or 'sweetheart' or..."

"My boy?" I stroke his cheeks with my thumbs and he nods, his head heavy in my hands.

"Yeah, that." His eyes are still closed and a faint pink blush stains his cheeks. "It makes me feel safe. And taken care of. And..." He squirms a little and shuffles closer to me.

"Hot because it's the good kind of dirty and wrong?" I supply.

He opens his eyes and looks up at me again. "Yeah."

Nine

LOGAN

"WE SHOULD TALK ABOUT RULES AND LIMITS, then," I say.

Silas makes a face. "Won't that just take all the fun out of it?"

"Consent is critical, Silas. And in order to consent to something, you have to know what you're consenting to. So far, you've agreed to stay the weekend and we've already talked about how you like it when you call me Daddy and I call you my boy."

"Don't you like it, too?" He takes a sip of his coffee and peers at me over the rim of his mug.

"I do, baby. Very much." More than I'm ready to tell him yet. "But my question is—do you want that only in relation to sex? Or do you want that outside of the bedroom as well?"

"So far, we've had more sex outside your bedroom than in it," Silas points out.

I shake my head with a smile. "Fair point. But my question stands."

I gather our breakfast dishes up and take them to the sink to give him a minute to think about it. I'm trying not to think too much about what I want. Because I could be happy with it just as a bedroom dynamic, but what I really want is Silas as my boy all the time.

Either way, I don't know how I'll be able to give him up after the weekend ends.

When I turn back to the island, Silas is dragging his coffee mug in a figure eight pattern on the marble countertop. "I dunno. I think...maybe...more than just during sex?"

It's more of a question than an answer, like he's afraid I'll think less of him if he confesses to what he really wants.

"Good," I say and Silas's face lights up like a beacon. "That's what I want, too. But there's still a lot we need to talk about, in terms of how that will work."

Silas makes another face, but I ignore it this time. I can't tell if he wants to be a brat sometimes, or if he's just doing it because he thinks I expect it. I'm going to let that unfold naturally, though, rather than force him to classify himself like that now.

"What's your exposure to the Daddy/boy lifestyle?" I ask him. "Have you had a Daddy before?"

A sudden, deeply disturbing thought occurs to me. Could he have done this with Lance? Called Lance Daddy? Or the reverse?

I glance up from washing the skillet and Silas's cheeks are a little pink. Definitely not the reverse. Silas is a boy through and through, not a Daddy. And not because of how he looks. I've seen twinks more feminine than him with serious Daddy energy.

But there's something about Silas's demeanor that begs someone to take care of him. If Silas asked Lance to take care of him like that...well, that's a thought I'm not interested in following to its logical conclusion.

Silas is playing with his coffee mug again. "I've never had a Daddy before, no."

Thank God. But that's not a complete answer to my question. "When I ask you a question, boy, I expect a complete and truthful answer." I finish washing the skillet and rest it in the drying rack. "If you haven't had a Daddy before, what do you know about the lifestyle and how did you learn about it?"

Silas blushes a fetching pink and hides behind his coffee mug. "Um, porn, mostly."

I snort. "Not the most accurate portrayal."

Silas gives me a look. "I know that. I've also been to a kink club with my friend, Chloe."

It's been so long since I've been in the scene that I don't bother asking which one. Whether I recognize the name of the club isn't as important as what Silas experienced there. "And you saw some Daddies and boys there?"

Silas nods. "There were some boys dressed in onesies and sucking on pacifiers. I'm not into that kind of stuff. I just want..." he trails off, looking unsure again.

"Someone to take care of you?"

"Yeah," he says. "I mean, I'm totally capable of taking care of myself."

"Of course you are, baby."

"I just want someone to take charge, you know?" He slides off the stool and brings his mug to the sink. "So I don't have to...I dunno...deal with stuff."

I dry my hands off, then pull Silas into my embrace. He leans his head against my shoulder and I kiss the top of it. His blond hair is silky under my lips. "There's nothing wrong with that, baby boy. I like taking care of you."

I hold him for a few moments, then kiss the top of his head again and let go.

"Here's my suggestion, sweetheart. You let me be your Daddy for the rest of the weekend and we'll see if that's something we both like." I'm confident I'll love it, but I want to give Silas an out if he doesn't.

Silas looks at me from under the fall of his bangs. "How would that be different from what we're already doing?" There's a cheeky smile lingering at the corners of his mouth and I can tell he's already sinking into the role.

"You let Daddy make all the decisions the rest of the weekend. You'll do as I say, whenever and however I say, and I'll take care of everything."

"Everything?"

I tuck his hair behind his ear and brush my thumb across his cheekbone. "I will never abuse your trust, baby boy. But that's what this is about. You deciding to trust that I'll take care of you and that all the decisions I make for you are for your benefit."

"And if it turns out I don't like it? You making all my decisions, I mean. I like the other stuff we've been doing."

He winks at me and I smile down at him. "Then you tell me you don't want to do it anymore and we stop. You're the one with the power here, sweetheart. It's yours to give or withhold as you wish."

"But what about if I say I don't want something but I really kind of do?"

"Kind of?" I raise an eyebrow at him.

Silas looks down and his cheeks pinken. "Sometimes I think I want something, but I'm not really sure if I'll like it if I do it."

"Are we talking about something specific?" I ask. I've already seen that Silas likes a little pain with his pleasure, and if he wants more pain than what I've been giving him so far, we can definitely negotiate that.

He shrugs and doesn't meet my eyes. "Not really. I mean, there's lots of stuff I've thought about, but Lance never wanted to try anything too weird or freaky." He glances up at me and rests his hand on my chest. "Sorry."

"What are you apologizing for?"

"Well, it's weird talking about this stuff with you and also talking about Lance."

Believe me, I know. I try to ignore the stab of guilt I feel that it's my kid who's hurt him—Lance is a grown man, if a deeply immature one, and I'm not responsible for his choices—and I wrap my arms around Silas and tuck his head into my chest.

"There's nothing wrong with you, baby," I say. Jesus, the insecurity of youth is so raw. I remember those days, when anything someone says to you makes you question everything about yourself. "You're perfect the way you are, sweetheart. You and Lance just aren't right for each other, that's all."

Understatement of the year. It's almost inevitable that your first love hurts you deeply. Silas will see that eventually. He'll get over Lance, like I got over the first boy who broke my heart, and he'll find someone who loves him for himself.

Silas heaves a sigh against my chest, then lifts his head. "I don't want to talk about Lance anymore. I don't even want to think about him. Or about anything else. I think I want..." He looks up and meets my eyes squarely. "Yeah, no, I do want you to take charge, Daddy. Please."

I cup his face in my hands and lean down to kiss him. A soft kiss, at first, but Silas opens for me and I chase the taste of coffee and cream in his mouth, our tongues tangling with wet heat.

"Good boy," I praise him when we surface for air. "We can try anything you want to this weekend. We can use the stop-light system. Green to keep going, yellow to slow down, and red for stop. How's that?"

Silas nods. "Yeah, that works."

I kiss him again and when I pull back, still cradling his face in my hands, Silas looks more relaxed than I've seen him so far. His eyes are half-closed and his lips slightly parted. "I'll take care of you, baby boy. All you have to do is what Daddy tells you. Trust Daddy to give you what you need."

It feels like a vow. A vow that it's far too soon to be making to this boy, who might have come to me precisely because he trusts me, but who also needs time to mend the heart my son broke.

I mean it, though. For as long as he lets me, I'll do everything in my power to take care of this boy.

Silas kisses me again. A close-mouthed, chaste kiss. The kind we might exchange if there were witnesses to the vow I just made. "Yes, Daddy. I will," he promises in return.

Ten

SILAS

I FEEL LIKE we should toast or something after that. It feels kind of major, like I just made a promise bigger than I realized. So, when Logan releases me, I pick up my nearly empty coffee mug and hold it out to him.

"To you, Daddy."

Logan picks his mug up and clinks the rim against mine. "To you, my baby boy."

"And to lots of hot, kinky sex this weekend," I add hopefully.

He shakes his head, but he also smiles at me. "To finishing these dishes first," he says.

I grab a dishtowel to dry the skillet and Logan returns to the subject of kinky sex. "Is there anything you know you don't like, Silas? Any hard limits?"

I rub the towel around and around the bottom of the skillet while I'm thinking. I honestly don't have that much sexual experience. Fumbled gropings and hasty blow jobs in high school. In college, my freshman roommate and I jerked each other off a few times. Then I met Lance and it's been all hand jobs and blow jobs in the two years we've been together. I mentioned something about him tying me up once—as a joke, to cover myself, in case he wasn't into it, and he laughed along with me and said something like, "yeah right, like that'll ever happen."

So, I don't really know what I like and what I don't like. I know what I like to watch in porn—bondage, rough sex, spankings. And there's some stuff that I'm not ready to mention to Logan yet.

There's also stuff that I skip over when I'm scrolling through the options.

"Bathroom stuff," I say. "I don't want to pee on you and I definitely don't want you to pee on me."

"No water sports," Logan says. "Check. What else?"

I think back to some of the kinkier stuff I've watched. I usually turn the sound way down, because while I like to watch what the dudes are doing, I don't always like to listen to what they're saying.

"I don't want to be called names," I say.

"Names?"

The skillet is dry as a bone by now but I keep rubbing the dish towel around the inside of it. "You know, like slut and come bucket and stuff like that."

"No verbal humiliation," Logan says. "Okay."

I set the skillet on the countertop. "Really? I mean, isn't that part of the whole Daddy/boy thing?" It always is in porn.

"Have I called you anything you don't like, Silas?"

"No," I admit. "I already told you I like it when you call me your baby boy."

"Or sweetheart, right?"

I nod. I like that almost as much.

"Some people like verbal humiliation and some people don't, Silas. It's not my preference, either, though if you really wanted it, I could probably find something that would work for both of us. But I much prefer treating you like the precious boy you are and not like a hole to use."

"But you will fuck my hole, won't you, Daddy? I mean, I want you to do that, I just don't want you to call me a dirty whore or whatever."

"Trust me, baby. I'll fuck your hole and call you my sweet boy the whole time."

He keeps saying that. *Trust me.*

I know I can. Trust him, I mean. I've known him for two years. Okay, so mostly as Lance's dad and not in the ways that we're getting to know each other this weekend. For instance, I didn't know he was a Daddy before this weekend. Or that he likes a boy to take care of.

Except... Didn't I?

There's a reason I picked Logan as my rebound fuck. I mean, other than as revenge because he's Lance's dad and because I've been attracted to him almost as long as I've known him.

He makes me feel safe. Safer than a random dude from a club, for sure, but also safe, like, I don't know, emotionally or whatever. Like I could tell him anything, including the freaky shit I think I might want in bed, and he wouldn't judge me.

Even more, he'd do his best to give it to me. I think I knew this even before I risked showing up on his doorstep.

Logan's always taken care of things. He's not controlling or anything, but when I've been here with Lance, Logan always makes sure that we eat healthy meals and drink enough water and put sunscreen on if we're going to spend the day hanging out by the pool.

He set up Lance's trust fund so that it paid for college and bought his apartment and all the bills are paid through it. I offered to pay rent when Lance asked me to move in with him, but Logan swooped in when he overheard that and insisted that I save my money. I don't even pay for my own cell phone plan anymore—Logan put me on his family data plan when Lance and I moved in together.

I suppose it's a good thing now that I did as he insisted, because I'm going to need that money to get my own place. At least I've got a little bit of a safety net. Not enough to get a place anywhere near as nice as Lance's condo, but probably enough for first and last month's rent and a security deposit on something that's smaller and in a cheaper neighborhood.

Logan comes up behind me and puts a hand on my back. "Where did you go, baby?"

I realize that I'm still standing in front of the dish rack, a damp dish towel in my hand, and I shake thoughts about what I'm going to do after this weekend away.

"Just thinking of you fucking my hole, Daddy." I drape the towel over the oven door handle. Then I back up and shimmy my ass against his groin. "Today, I hope."

"We'll see," Logan says, infuriatingly noncommittal.

The doorbell rings and I honest to god jump at the sound. Oh, shit. Is it one of Logan's neighbors? Or Lance? There's no reason for him to be here, except that this is his dad's house and his childhood home and it's nearly Christmas and why shouldn't he come see his dad?

He has more right to be here than I do.

My heart starts to pound and I realize I'm gripping the oven door handle like I'm going to tear it off. I'm standing in his dad's kitchen on a Saturday morning, barefoot, and with the last vestiges of our breakfast in the sink.

I'm dressed, at least, and I'm wearing my own jeans, but also a shirt that belongs to his dad. And while Logan's fully dressed, too, and doesn't look like he spent last night getting me off half a dozen ways, we both know what we did.

I cast a panicked look around the kitchen. I could turn the corner and go down the hall, but that leads to Lance's bedroom. There's a guest room next to his—I could hide there, I suppose? Or maybe I should go downstairs? But that's another open space with a huge flat-screen TV bolted to the wall, a big comfy sectional, a piano that I've never heard either Lance or Logan play, and some gym equipment.

Hiding upstairs in Logan's bedroom is probably the safest bet, but oh my god, how fucked up is that?

Logan puts a hand on my back. "Silas. It's a delivery. Relax."

He kisses the side of my head like no big deal and crosses to answer the door. I can't see who it is from where I'm standing when he swings the door open, but I hear a murmured "thanks" from Logan and the rustle of a paper bag changing hands.

Logan closes the door and turns around. He crosses the living room and sets the paper bag on the coffee table, then looks toward where I'm still standing frozen in the kitchen. "Silas, come here."

Holy shit, how have I never noticed how many windows Logan's house has? The back wall of the living room is basically entirely windows with a sliding glass door that leads out to the back deck. The opposite wall is windowed, too, and the front door also has a big window in the middle of it. The dining room on the other side of the fireplace divider is freaking three walls of floor to ceiling transparent glass.

Anyone could have looked in and seen what we were doing last night. I was sprawled out naked on the couch. Logan fucked my face and I sucked him off. And his neighbors could have seen *everything*. That delivery person could have seen us, too, if they'd arrived while Logan was fucking me. Which I'd just asked him to do.

"Silas," Logan says again. "Don't make me repeat myself, boy."

I force my leaden legs to leave the relative safety of the kitchen and join him in the living room. He reaches out a long arm and draws me to him. "What's the matter, baby?"

I tuck my burning face into his chest and let him put his arms around me. "I just...what if your neighbors see us this weekend?" I've met some of Logan's neighbors. Mrs. White lives next door. She's in her seventies, at least, and Logan shovels snow from her driveway and does other odd jobs for her when her grown children aren't available. She and I talk about the arts a lot—she was a dancer when she was young and I majored in theater at NYU. She knows I'm Lance's boyfriend.

Or was.

"How will the neighbors see us, Silas?" Logan crooks his knuckle under my chin and lifts my face. I look out each set of windows. There's a privacy fence along the property line at the side yard and landscaped trees and shrubs in the backyard. There's a row of mature arborvitae trees between the front yard and Mrs. White's driveway.

Oh. I take a deep breath. "Okay, right."

My heart rate has slowed a little and I'm no longer about to hyperventilate. But then Logan looks me dead in the eyes and says, "Even if they did, what they'd see is how beautiful my boy is and how much I enjoy taking care of him."

He kisses me, overriding my embarrassment and fear. Then he presses a hot line of kisses along my neck, and whispers in between, "I don't care who sees us, baby. If it were warmer, I'd lay you out on the back deck and have you any way I want. I'd fuck you in a lounge chair, and in the pool, and in the grass. I'd make you take your Daddy's cock in your mouth and in your ass until you can't take it anymore."

He holds the back of my head in a hard grip and thrusts his tongue into my mouth. "And anyone who wants to watch is welcome to."

Oh my god. A rush of humiliation and arousal burns through me like fire. I told Logan that I didn't want to be called filthy names, but this scenario—being put on display, forced to take whatever my Daddy wants to give me—yeah, I could get behind that.

"Yes, Daddy. Please." I'm gasping and whimpering and Logan is nipping at my earlobes and sucking hard kisses into my neck. He's grinding his erection against mine and there are too many clothes between us. I pluck at the tail of his sweater, trying to get my hands under it, under his shirt, on his skin.

The freaking doorbell rings again, interrupting us. Logan musses my hair with his big hand before letting me go to answer it. He swings the door wide open enough that another delivery person can look in and see me. My lips puffy from Logan's kisses, my hair probably looking like I just got out of bed.

The delivery guy doesn't look at me, though. He barely looks at Logan—just hands over two large tote bags and jogs down the walk to the small truck idling in the driveway.

Logan puts the groceries away and I try to get over my freakout. And the hard-on that he caused when he talked about fucking me in full view of anyone who wanted to watch us.

When he closes the refrigerator door on the last of the groceries, he comes back to the living room, parks himself in the middle of the couch, and gestures at the paper bag he'd left on the coffee table.

"Wouldn't you like to see what else I had delivered for us?"

Eleven

LOGAN

SILAS'S EYES WIDEN and then dart to the brown paper bag. "For us? What is it?"

I crook my finger and motion for him to sit next to me. "Open it and see."

He reaches for the bag and pulls out the first item. He hefts the sixteen ounce bottle of lube in one hand and looks sideways at me. "Planning to use all of it this weekend?"

I shrug. "I was an Eagle Scout. I still believe in being prepared."

He gives me a delighted grin, then pulls two boxes from the bag. One is black and shaped like an oversized jewelry box. "Open that one first," I tell him.

He slips the cardboard sleeve off and lifts the lid. Nestled in hot pink satin in a space molded to fit is a stainless steel butt plug. Its large head is vaguely heart-shaped and it has a tapered stem that ends in a ring. It's shiny and smooth and Silas's eyes light up.

He touches the plug lightly with a finger and looks at me. "Think you can keep that in you for a while today?" I ask him. It will open him up and get him ready for my cock later.

"Yes, Daddy," he breathes, his eyes drawn back to the plug.

"Good boy."

His fingers go to the buttons on his jeans. "Can I? Now?"

I want him to wear what's in the other box, too, but I'm happy to plug his ass before I show him what else I've got in store for him. "Of course, baby. Let me just clean it first." When I return, he rocks onto his back on the sofa and lifts his hips enough to shimmy his jeans and underwear down to expose his ass. "Just like that, baby," I tell him when he gets the cloth around mid-thigh. I can see the shadowed cleft of his hole under his balls and I push his knees toward his chest.

He cooperates by wrapping his arms around his legs and hugging them close. I crack open the lube and squeeze a dollop on the tip of the plug, then smear it all around the head. I slip my fingers between his cheeks and find his hole, circling and spreading the lube around it. Silas draws his knees up farther, giving me better access.

I line the plug up and press gently. It slides in as easy as can be and Silas moans as it goes in. "That's it, baby boy," I say. The ring nestles between his cheeks until he lets go of his legs and I can't see it anymore.

But I know it's there, and Silas clearly does, too. He plants his feet on the sofa cushion and wiggles his hips a few times. "How does it feel?" I ask.

"Full," he says. "Is this what it will feel like to take your cock, Daddy?"

His knees fall sideways and I can see that his cock is hard and the pearl bead of the piercing through the head is glistening with pre-come.

I chuckle and pat his knee. "You'll have to let me know when it comes to that, baby. I think I'm a little bigger than that plug, though."

"Good," he says. "Because I know I can take more, Daddy. I want to take all of you."

Christ, he's such a good boy for me. I let him squirm around on the sofa, testing the feel of the plug inside him. He makes whimpering sounds in the back of his throat and he's probably mere moments away from coming, but I've got a solution for that.

"Sit up, sweetheart. Don't you want your other present?"

I help him tug his jeans and underwear up over his ass but keep the fly open and his cock exposed. I pull him upright next to me and watch his face as I hand him the other box.

He opens it and stares down at the contents. The concentric metal rings gleam in the winter sunlight filtering through the southern wall of windows in the living room. His blond brows draw together and he plucks the metal contraption from the box, turning it over in his hand.

"Holy shit," he breathes. He darts a quick glance at me, but his eyes go right back to the cage. "Really?"

"If you're okay with it, baby. You can say no."

"No," he says immediately, then looks up at me with wide eyes. "I mean, no, I don't want to say no. I mean, yes, I'm okay with it. More than okay." His words are tumbling out and his eagerness to please is such a fucking turn on. I'm as hard as he is right now and I have to adjust myself. Something that Silas doesn't even notice, because he's still turning the cock cage over in his hands.

Then he holds it next to his cock like he's comparing them. "Don't think it's gonna fit, though," he says with a cheeky grin. The cage is just over two and a half inches long and he is quite a bit longer than that.

But there's one sure-fire way to get his erection to go down. And he's been such a good boy.

I push the coffee table back from the sofa and get down on the floor. This is going to be hell on my knees, but worth it. I doubt it'll take very long, anyway.

His eyes widen at the sight of me on my knees for him. "Oh, fuck," he says faintly when I suck as much of him down as I can in one go.

His hips thrust up as soon as I get my mouth on him and he groans loud and long above me. It doesn't take long at all. His Prince Albert piercing barely grazes the back of my throat and he's shooting his load down it. I swallow hastily—I'd really rather not have to clean come off the sofa cushions—and keep his cock in my mouth until he finishes spurting. He slumps bonelessly, his thighs spreading as much as his tight jeans will let them.

When I pull off him, his cock is small and pink, shiny from spit and come. I push up to my feet and wince at the crack my left knee gives and grab some wet wipes from the downstairs bathroom. Silas twitches a little at the cold wetness, but lets me take care of him.

When he's clean, I take the cage from his unresisting hand and gently scoop his balls through the ring and into the cage. I tuck his flaccid penis into place, mindful of the ladder of piercings, and close the cage, then insert the bolt and tighten it with the Allen wrench.

I chose this model because I like the rings and how it encloses his balls, too, and because I didn't want to freak him out by literally locking him away with a padlock and keys that could be lost. I don't own him, even though I'd like to. For now, I love the look of him, so small and sweet, tucked away like a gift for me to unwrap later.

"Oh," he says on a soft exhalation and his head falls back against the sofa back.

My hands flutter around the cage. "There's a hinge at the back, behind your balls. Is it hurting you, baby?"

He shakes his head. His eyes are closed and there's a quiet peacefulness on his face that's tinged with a flush of arousal. He isn't hard—he can't get hard, thanks to the cage—but he looks like he's seconds from coming without the strain of reaching for it.

Twelve

SILAS

"OH, Daddy," I say. I open my eyes to look at Logan and his eyebrows are drawn together. He looks almost fatherly again, and it turns my crank all the way round.

"I love it. It's so…" I wiggle a little to jostle the plug inside my ass and a fresh wave of arousal floods through my entire body. It stops at my crotch, though, blood pooling at the base of my dick because it can't get me hard and holy fucking shit, this is the most amazing thing I've ever felt.

Logan's eyebrows unknit and he smiles at me. He cups my cock and balls in the cage in his hand. My entire package fits within the curve of his hand and I can feel my pulse in my groin, thudding deeply.

Logan looks darkly satisfied and his thumb strokes my soft dick through the rings. "So pretty, sweetheart," he says.

We sit there for a few minutes while I drift in the competing sensations of the fullness in my ass and the blood trying to fill my cock. I'm staring blindly down at my crotch and Logan is still holding me gently, tracing around the rings with butterfly touches, like I'm a delicate flower. It's intense, but also freeing, and I slowly relax until my arms and legs are resting limply where they fall.

"Okay, baby?" Logan finally asks. I nod and he pulls me to my feet, then helps me tug my underwear and jeans up over my caged cock. It's a bit of a struggle to get the buttons fastened over the bulge of the cage, but the jeans have a bit of stretch to them and I leave it to my Daddy to manage.

He tucks the Allen wrench into the front pocket of my jeans and I stand there for a minute, shifting from foot to foot, testing the feel of being upright with a metal plug in my ass and a metal cage enclosing my junk.

It's strange, but not uncomfortable. I look at Logan, who's standing at the end of the couch, watching me. Then he crosses the living room, around the fireplace divider, and heads into the dining room. "Wait," I say. "Aren't we going to...?"

"Come here, sweetheart."

The weight of both plug and cage makes me feel like I'm about to melt into a puddle, but I force my legs to move. With every step, my ass clenches around the plug and lightning flares up my spine.

When I reach the dining room, Logan pulls a chair out for me and I sit. It's easy to just do what he says. More than easy.

I could really get used to this. Even though I know I shouldn't.

Logan takes the seat to my left, at the head of the table. He clicks the remote control to the gas fireplace and the flames whoosh on. Then he settles his glasses on his face and peers at the half-finished jigsaw puzzle spread out on the table.

"Really?" I ask. "Now?"

Logan always has a jigsaw puzzle going. He likes the really complicated kind, with a thousand pieces and complicated artwork, but he sometimes does smaller and simpler ones too. I think it started when Lance was a kid, as something they could do together that wasn't video games. But Lance gets bored easily and quit doing puzzles with his dad long before we met.

I love jigsaw puzzles, though. The first weekend Lance brought me here to get to know his dad, Logan had a puzzle going that looked like a vintage advertisement for some sort of

Belgian beer. Logan and Lance were arguing over what movie we should watch and I sort of drifted over to the puzzle table. The border was almost complete, only the right side missing one piece to join it all up. The edge pieces were this dark brown color that shaded to a deep purple and I saw that a few of the pieces were connected to adjoining pieces that looked like they fit but didn't quite. I swapped a few pieces around, then snapped the edge together, completing the puzzle's frame.

Then Lance called my name, and I looked over, suddenly feeling guilty for having rearranged pieces of Logan's puzzle without asking.

"Uh, sorry. What'd you say?"

Logan crossed the room and looked from me to the puzzle and back again. "I've been trying to finish that edge for days," he said. "Well done." Then he smiled at me, this quiet, private smile that excluded Lance and made me feel like I'd done something to make him proud.

It was stupid—all I'd done was notice that the colors of the misaligned pieces didn't quite match—but I think now it was the start of things with Logan. I've been craving that approving smile ever since.

In the two years I dated Lance, I spent a lot of evenings working on a puzzle with Logan while Lance watched sports on the wide-screen TV bolted to the wall above the fireplace.

I've never done a puzzle with a cock cage on my dick and a plug in my ass, though.

I settle gingerly on the upholstered chair and take the puzzle's lid to look at the picture. It's a seaside scene of a coastal town in Maine. There's a red-and-white-striped lighthouse in the top right corner and the light keeper's squat house nestled at the foot of the lighthouse. There's a pile of red lobsters, white clams, and bluish oysters in the middle of the picture, on a wooden dock that stretches across blue water, and a windswept rocky coastline with waves crashing over dark boulders in the bottom right corner. In the bottom left, there are blueberry bushes and foliage in a mix of greens and golds.

The sky in the top portion of the picture is streaked with pink and purple, like the sun has just dropped below the horizon.

Logan's got most of the edge pieces in place and a good start on the lighthouse. I start picking through the pieces in the box, looking for bits of red lobster, white clams, and the blueberries.

Logan told me once that he does puzzles to let his mind wander and think about things. He's figured out solutions to his clients' legal issues while puzzling and when he's stressed at work, he sometimes stays up late working on a puzzle rather than working late at the office.

There's something calming about sorting through the pieces, dividing them up by color and figuring out which piece goes where. Plus, there's the satisfaction of snapping a piece into the right place and watching the art take shape before your eyes. I don't forget about the plug or the cage, but the urgency of wanting Logan to fuck me gradually recedes to the back of my mind.

Out of the blue, Logan asks, "Do you have the book for your musical and any of the songs on your phone? Or saved in the cloud that you can access from here?"

Logan's voice is deep and it's got this warm quality to it, like melted chocolate. I could listen to him read a shopping list, so it takes a minute for his question to register. "What?"

"Do you?"

"Um, yeah. Why?"

"Send them to me," Logan says.

"Now? Why?" I feel a little like a broken record.

"Because I'm asking you to." Logan looks implacable. His lips are in a firm line and his eyes aren't showing the crinkles at the corners that he gets when he smiles. It's his professional face—the one I've seen dozens of times when I've spied on him while he's working. Like he's questioning a witness on the stand and waiting to hear whether they'll tell the truth or not.

"Okay." I shrug. I did agree to do what he tells me to do this weekend. I've got no idea what he wants with my musical, but I do trust him. Even with my creative work.

Logan finds my phone and hands it to me. Shit, there are fifteen unread texts and two missed calls. From Chloe, mostly, and she did say that if I didn't call her in the morning, she'd track my location and find me. She would, too. She's paranoid about safety.

I mean, I guess you can't call it paranoid to be concerned about safety when you engage in the kind of kinky shit she does. And she knows that I don't go home with random dudes. Logan's not a random dude, but I didn't tell her who I was with last night, just that I was safe. Crap, I hope she believed me.

One of the missed calls is from Lance. Which I am not returning. Lance can go fuck himself. Or whatever new dude he randomly comes across.

I glance up at Logan, torn between dealing with Chloe and doing what he told me to do. "I gotta call my friend."

He gets up and bends to kiss my forehead. "Send me the files first, then call your friend. I'll go upstairs and do some work, so you can take as much time as you need."

"Yes, Daddy." He stands over me until I email him the book and a couple of music files.

"Good boy," he says.

When I hear his tread on the stairs, I call Chloe, who picks up on the first ring.

"Where the fuck are you, Silas?" she demands. "I've been worried sick about you. Your phone location says you're in Westport, but *do not* tell me you're making up with that cheating asshole. He's supposed to be your ex, remember? That slimy turd goblin."

I snort. Chloe's got the most creative range of insults of anyone I've ever met. And she never uses the same combination twice. It's impressive, truly.

"I'm not making up with Lance," I tell her.

"Then what the hell are you doing in Westport? The only reason you ever used to go there was to spend weekends at that stupid douche pirate's dad's house."

"Yeah," I say. "I, um, came out here last night. On the train. Then I took an Uber to Logan's house."

"Logan's house? Who the fuck is Logan?"

Oh, right. I don't think I've ever told Chloe Logan's first name. I lower my voice to a whisper. "Um...Mr. Reynolds. Lance's dad."

There's a brief silence, then Chloe takes a deep breath through her nose that I can hear and says, "Silas, why did you spend the night at Mr. Reynolds' house?"

"Um...revenge?" There's a lift at the end of my sentence and I'd like to think she hears it as sarcasm, but it's hard to pull shit over on Chloe.

"Revenge?" Chloe echoes. "What kind of revenge?"

There's a moment of silence while I think of how to explain, and then Chloe shrieks in my ear. "Oh my god! Did you fuck him?"

"Um...sort of?"

"Sort of? Holy shit, Silas, how do you sort of fuck somebody?"

"Okay, fine. Yes, I fucked him. I mean, not *fucked* him fucked him—we haven't gotten to that yet. But he sucked me off and I sucked him off and we—well, anyway, you don't need to know the details."

"Oh, I'm gonna need to hear all the details when you get back, dude. Don't think you can hold out on me."

I am not telling her about coming just from Logan playing with my nipples. And I sure as hell am not telling her about the cage or the plug or the Daddy/boy stuff. Not that she would judge—she knows I might be into that and she's the queen of live and let others have their kinks. But it's temporary and feels too fragile to talk about yet.

Like having Logan as my Daddy is a big, shimmery soap bubble hovering in the air in front of me and if I do or say anything to disturb it, it will pop and disappear forever.

I mean, it's only for the weekend, so it'll disappear no matter what. Gotta remember that.

"Whoa," Chloe is saying. "I mean, I knew you've had the hots for him for a while, but I wouldn't have expected you to actually follow through on it. That's ballsy, dude."

"Thanks," I say dryly. "Wait, how did you know I have the hots for him?"

"Dude, it's obvious. The way you talk about him. *Mr. Reynolds is working on this important case and he said*...blah, blah, blah."

"What? I don't talk about him like that."

"Yeah, right. You get this look on your face when you talk about him. Like you're imagining being on your knees for him and loving every minute of it."

"Jesus," I say, covering my eyes with my hand. "I hope Lance never noticed that."

Chloe snorts. "That tone-deaf shart hound wouldn't notice how you feel about anything if you wrote it on poster board and held it up in front of his face."

Chloe's a huge fan of that star-studded Christmas movie where one of the characters holds up posters declaring his love for another character while playing *Silent Night* on a CD player outside her door. I, personally, think that scene is creepy as fuck. He declares his undying love for his best friend's wife after being a dick to her the whole movie and that's romantic? And then she runs down the steps and kisses him? What if her husband had answered the door?

Anyway, Chloe's creative insults and crappy taste in movies aside, she's not wrong about Lance. He probably never noticed anything between me and Logan. It's not like we ever did anything to notice anyway.

"Wait, whose idea was this? How did this happen? Did he come on to you? Are you sure this is what you want?"

"Um...mine, I showed up at his door last night and seduced him, so no, and it's only for this weekend, so it's no big deal."

"No big deal? Silas, I know I'm the one who told you that a little rebound fuck might help you get over Lance, but fucking his dad? I mean, that's a little...I don't know..."

"Incestuous?" I put in with a slightly deranged giggle. "Oh no, it can't be that, remember, because it's not like Lance ever asked me to marry him. So Logan isn't my father-in-law and never will be."

"You don't want to marry that insecure ass clown, Silas. I'm just saying maybe you need some time to get over him before you jump into something serious."

"Who said anything about serious, Chloe? I told you this is just for the weekend."

"Okay, okay." She sounds doubtful, but whatever, she's not the boss of me. And now I'm thinking about how I'm letting Logan be the boss of me this weekend, and I'm ready to get off the phone and get back to him.

"I gotta go, Chlo, I'll see you in a couple of days."

"Be safe, Silas. Don't do anything I wouldn't do."

"That really doesn't leave much out, does it?" Chloe's very much a I'll-try-anything-once kind of girl.

"Guess not," she snickers. "Just...be careful, hon, okay? And text me when you're heading back to the city."

"I will," I promise. I'm already hanging up and heading for the stairs. To Logan.

Thirteen

LOGAN

I TOLD SILAS I'd do some work while he talked with his friend, but all I do is skim through the previews of a dozen or so unread emails to make sure there's nothing I need to handle today.

And open the message Silas sent me, with his musical files attached. I forward the email to James Cohen and append a quick note, then lean back in my chair.

What the fuck am I doing? Playing with a boy young enough to be my son. Who was *dating* my son, for Christ's sake.

Letting him call me Daddy. Spinning out every dirty fantasy I've had since I met him. Caging his cock, plugging his ass to stretch him for mine. I haven't fucked him—I haven't crossed that line yet—but the real line was crossed when I put my hand around his throat last night.

Or maybe I crossed it when I let him rub his face over my cock in the taxi and feel how hard I was. I should have lifted him off my lap before he noticed. I should have sent him home last night. Or put him up in Lance's bedroom, or the guest room. Or let him crash on the sofa, for fuck's sake. Anywhere but in my bed.

Except that the home he had was with my son, who cheated on him. And the responsibility I feel to make up for my son's betrayal is all tangled up in how much I want him.

How much I want to keep him in my life, even after Lance cast him aside. I want to fuck him—it's terrifying how much I want to fuck him—but I've also always genuinely liked Silas. Having breakfast together, talking about his musical, working on the puzzle together—all these small interactions with him that I'll lose when he gets his revenge and moves on with his life.

I scrub my hands over my face. Jesus, what kind of a sick fuck am I that I'm willing to trade on Silas's natural desire for revenge just so I get to spend a few more days with him? I should encourage him to grieve the end of his relationship, take time to get over Lance, and then—when he's ready—find someone closer to his age.

Not push him into a kinky scenario that only exacerbates the power differential between us. That he's likely too emotionally distraught to truly consent to.

But I saw the peaceful expression on his face when he agreed to be my boy for the weekend. And how his whole body relaxed when I put the cage on his cock. Silas doesn't hide his feelings well, at all. He wasn't faking either reaction. I don't think he could, even if he wanted to.

It doesn't make what I'm doing with him right, but damn if it doesn't feel more right than anything I've ever done.

There's a soft tap on my half-closed office door and Silas peeks his head around it. I close the lid of my laptop and motion that he can come in.

"Hi, sweetheart. Done with your friend?"

He nods and takes small steps into the room. Right. He's still locked in the cock cage and he's still got the plug inside him. It's been longer than I'd planned, and I'm aching to lay him out and see him prepped and ready for me.

Maybe not on my desk, though.

And then Silas melts to the floor like he can't stand up any longer and crawls on hands and knees around my desk. I swivel my chair to face him and he comes up in between my knees. His cheeks are pink and his lips red and puffy, like he's been biting them. He shimmies closer and puts his elbows on my thighs.

"Hi, Daddy."

"Hi, baby." He looks expectant, and all the agonizing and self-recrimination I've been stewing in seems like not just a waste of time, but ungrateful when I have this precious boy on his knees before me, waiting to please me. *Wanting* to please me. "Would you like to suck Daddy's cock?"

Silas grins. "Hell, yeah. I thought you'd never ask."

His hands reach for my slacks and make quick work of the button and zip. He gets my cock out and his mouth immediately engulfs it. I run my fingers through his hair and clasp my hands at the base of his skull.

I hold his head lightly and let him set the pace. Until he gets really into it and he's taking more and more of my cock down his throat. His tongue piercing scrapes the underside of my cock and his mouth is hot and wet and perfect. The next time he goes down, I hold him there, my hands pressing down on his head, the heels of my palms squeezing his neck.

I can feel air blowing in and out of his nostrils at the base of my cock and the soft give of his throat is going to make me come sooner than I'd expected. I let him up for air once and he sucks in a quick gulp, his eyes blinking around tears in his lashes. Then I force his head down again and hold him still while I pump short, quick jerks of my hips, up and up and up, into his throat. The choking noises he makes while I unload make my orgasm feel like it lasts longer than normal.

When I stop pulsing into Silas's throat, I let go of his head and he pulls off my softening cock with a huge gasp for air. He's got one elbow digging into the muscle of my inner thigh, bracing himself, while his back curls forward and he coughs wetly into his other hand.

I dig awkwardly into the pocket of my slacks for a handkerchief and hand it to him. "If you get come on my rug, I'll stripe your ass hard enough you won't sit comfortably for a week, boy."

I don't mean it. I just damn near choked him with my cock and if a little come drips onto the rug, I'll clean it up later. But he looks up at me with his face shiny from tears and snot and come and grins a white-spattered toothy grin at me. "No, Daddy, I wouldn't do that."

His eyes are shining like he's just been given the best present he could think of. Then his back curls forward again and he coughs into the handkerchief some more.

I stroke his hair until he settles and rests his head on my thigh. Then I gently grasp his upper arms, lifting him off me, and push my chair back. "I'll get something to clean you up, sweetheart."

He nods and sort of slumps sideways, leaning against my desk. When I come back from the kitchen with wet wipes and a glass of chocolate soy milk, he's sprawled on his back on the floor.

I set the wet wipes and the glass on my desk and perch on the corner of it. "Come here, baby. Let's clean you up."

He rolls over and pushes himself up to his knees by my desk, his ass resting on his heels. He lifts his face and I clean it with wet wipes, scrubbing the come and tear tracks from his cheeks.

"My eyelashes are sticky," he says.

"Which eye?"

He blinks a couple of times and I can see the lashes clump together. "Both of them."

I take a corner of wet wipe and scrub gently at his lashes until they separate. "Better?"

"Mmm, yeah. Thank you, Daddy."

He leans his head against my knee and I stroke his head, letting the silky strands run through my fingers.

"You're such a good boy for me, Silas."

He nuzzles his cheek against my knee and I could stay here for the rest of the afternoon, but it's past time to take the cage off. I tap the back of his head. "Up you go, baby."

"Don't wanna," he says and he sounds sleepy and content.

"You don't want to go to my bedroom?"

Silas pops his head up, suddenly alert. "Oh! No, I definitely want that. Are you finally going to fuck me, Daddy?"

Fourteen

SILAS

"WE'LL SEE," IS all Logan says. Which is infuriating, because why else am I wearing this butt plug, if not to stretch me so I can take his dick?

I mean, not that I haven't enjoyed having it in me. It jostles inside every time I move and lights my nerves up. It doesn't feel as full as when Logan first put it in me, so I suppose I've adjusted to it. Which is the point, right?

Logan motions for me to leave his office before him. I put a little extra sway in my hips and whoa, that jostles the plug even more inside me, so I keep doing it. Logan grabs one ass cheek and squeezes, which halts my steps halfway out the door, but he lets go quickly and swats my ass.

"Let's go, boy. Quit dawdling," he says.

The firm command in his deep voice makes my nipples tighten. My cock tries to fill, but it can't because I'm still wearing the cage. I'd sort of gotten used to it while we were working on the puzzle downstairs, but now all my attention is back at the base of my dick, where everything is just swirling deep in my pelvis and I go a little lightheaded.

I misjudge a step and stumble, but Logan's there to catch me. He wraps one arm around my waist and practically carries me into his bedroom. He lays me on the bed, on my back, and bends over me.

"Come on, baby, let's get these off you." He unbuttons my jeans and I try to help, but he just bats my hands away, so I let them fall by my sides and just float on his bed while he strips me naked.

He pushes my legs apart and kneels up on the bed between them. His hands rest on my pelvis, large and warm, and he's framing my caged dick, staring down at me.

"So pretty, baby," he murmurs. "All wrapped up, so soft and sweet, like a present, just for me."

He slides down so he's lying between my legs. All I can see is his head hovering over my hips, the dark and silver strands of his hair mussed together. Then his hot breath blows over my dick and he licks between the metal rings. "All for me," he whispers into the crease at my inner thigh. "Isn't that right, Silas?"

I nod my head against the pillows, though I don't know if he sees it. "For you, Daddy," I say. For the weekend, anyway. I close my eyes and pretend he really means it.

Logan licks at my skin in between every ring. Each time, there's a puff of hot air and his lips move against where the metal squeezes around me. It's probably my imagination— wishful thinking and all—but I can feel the word he mouths each time he licks at me.

Mine.

I'm clenching my hands and tossing my head around on the pillow. Logan's holding my hips, fingers drilling into them, elbows braced on the insides of my spread thighs, keeping me spread open and still for him. "Take it off, Daddy, *please*," I beg. I can't take much more of this torture.

His tongue disappears and his head lifts, then he lets go of me and sits up. "I decide how long you wear the cage and when it comes off. Understand?"

My hips lift, like my caged dick is a magnet to his mouth. He sits back on his heels and crosses his arms over his chest.

He's still dressed, except for his shoes, and at some point he'd done his pants up again after I sucked him.

"Yes, Daddy," I breathe.

He looks down at me, his eyes roaming over my flushed face, my heaving chest, my spread legs, and finally my caged dick and balls. He looks at me like he owns me. Like he'll do whatever he wants to me and my only job is to take it.

And as if his expression gives me a gentle push off a cliff, I tip from a shaking, desperate-to-come mess into peace.

My muscles relax, my hips settle on the mattress, and my legs fall open like my bones have melted. Logan smiles at me. "That's it, baby."

His hands are warm between my inner thighs and he's doing something down there, but I don't really notice or care what it is until I feel a breath of air against my cock and balls and realize that he's removing the cage.

I let out a little moan as all the blood the cage had constricted rushes south. Logan wraps his fingers around my balls and tugs a little, and oh shit, I'm coming. The pent-up jizz erupts from my dick in thick spurts but I'm still and peaceful even while my orgasm rushes over me.

Logan lets go of my nuts when I start spurting and watches me while my dick is throbbing and pulsing. I clench my ass to feel the plug shift inside me and another wave of electric tingles washes over me. My cock jerks once more and a weak spurt of come dribbles down my shaft.

"Sorry, Daddy," I say, and I give him my best sexy-sweet look. I don't know how successful I am, because he just looks at me without changing his expression.

"What are you sorry for?"

I probably shouldn't have come without permission, right? But I couldn't stop it. I lift my hand and flap it vaguely at the mess I've made all over my stomach. My arm is heavy and I let it flop back on the mattress next to me. "Didn't mean to, Daddy. You're just so hot." I hope I haven't gotten any come on his pants, but it's too much effort to angle my head to check.

Something in his face softens. "You're fine, sweetheart," he says. He gets off the bed and disappears for a minute, then returns with more wet wipes and mops the come off my skin. Again.

When he tosses the wipes in the wastebasket and sits on the bed, I turn onto my side and snuggle next to him with my back along his thigh. He puts a hand on my ribcage. His fingers slot in between my ribs and his thumb strokes up and down my spine.

"When was the last time you ate?" he asks, and oh wow, that note of fatherly concern that makes my knees weak rushes back.

"This morning, remember?" I say. "You made me eggs and bacon. And toast."

"And before then?"

I give a half-shrug. I've still got the plug in me and I'm sort of wondering if I should take it out, but it seems like a lot of work right now when I could be just lying here and letting Logan pet me like a kitten. Soft, delicate strokes whisper up and down my side. Like he's afraid he'll hurt me if he's too rough with me.

Which is a total contrast to how hard he fucked my face earlier. I could get used to this. Probably shouldn't. Logan will surely get tired of me disrupting his carefully ordered life soon.

But this weekend was his suggestion, so I'll just enjoy it as long as I can.

I turn over halfway and open my mouth to say something, but Logan shushes me. "It's all right, baby boy. You've clearly not been getting enough sleep. You take a nap."

He rolls me back onto my side and his warm hands stroke down my back before he pulls my ass cheeks apart and slowly tugs the plug free. He cleans the residual lube with another wet wipe and I flinch a little because it's kind of cold, but he's quick about it. Then he tucks me under the sheets and blankets.

"Will you stay?" I murmur, already on the edge of sleep, and he kisses the side of my head.

"Of course, baby boy. Until you're asleep."

There's rustling behind me and then Logan slips under the covers, the soft cotton of his undershirt and boxer briefs nice against my bare skin. He fits himself behind me, spooning me, and drapes a heavy arm over me. I take a deep breath of Logan's scent surrounding me, from his sheets and pillows to the smell of his shampoo and warm skin, and let myself fall asleep.

Fifteen

SILAS

WHEN I WAKE UP, I'm alone in bed and the angle of the pale winter sun through the curtains suggests it's late afternoon. How long have I slept?

I sit up and look around the bedroom. Logan folded my jeans and his long-sleeved shirt on the top of his dresser. I put them back on and head downstairs.

Logan's in the living room, pretty much where he was when I knocked on his door last night. He's got his reading glasses on again and his laptop balanced on his thighs. He looks up immediately when I enter the room.

"There's my boy. Did you sleep well?"

I nod and rub a bit of sleep crust from my eyes. "I'm sorry."

"What are you sorry for?" He shifts the computer from his lap to the coffee table, takes off his reading glasses, and sets them next to the laptop.

"For wasting part of our weekend together. I just haven't been sleeping well lately, so I guess between that and the orgasm..."

"Don't apologize for needing sleep, Silas. You need to take better care of yourself."

You're not my dad, is the first thing that pops into my mind. But isn't that what I said I wanted from Logan? Maybe I only want to call him Daddy during sex after all. I've been calling him Daddy a lot since I've been here, but we've mostly been doing sex-related stuff, even when doing other, normal things, too.

Although he made me sit and do a jigsaw puzzle with a cage on my cock and a plug up my ass. That's not exactly normal.

Or maybe it is, for Daddies and their boys. How the hell would I know?

I'm too groggy from my nap to process all this right now.

"Drink some water, Silas, and we'll make dinner in a bit."

"You're not the boss of me," I say, aloud, the words slipping out almost without my meaning to say them.

Logan pauses in the act of reaching for his laptop and looks up at me. "We agreed that I would be, didn't we?"

"For the weekend, yeah. But—"

"But what?" Logan settles back against the couch cushions and folds his arms over his chest. "Are you red?"

"What?" Oh, right. His stoplight system. Red for stop. Do I want to stop?

"I'm not a kid. I can decide for myself when I want to drink water."

I've got a dull headache throbbing under my right eye. Honestly, drinking some water would probably be a good idea. But I'm feeling cranky and unsettled and I don't know what the hell's wrong with me, but I can't seem to snap out of it.

"You're not a kid," Logan agrees. "But you're acting like a brat. If it's punishment you want, that can be arranged."

Wait, what? What does Logan mean by punishment? My dick seems to have a general idea, because it perks up.

"Screw that," I say, ignoring the traitor in my jeans.

Logan stands up and crosses the distance between us in a few strides. "I won't do this with you if you're not willing, Silas. Say 'red' and it ends now. I'll drive you to the train station or make you dinner and you can sleep in the guest room. Your choice."

Yeah, I don't like either of those choices. I don't want this to end. I don't know how to tell him that, though. So I don't say anything. I just stare up at him.

He grabs my upper arm and squeezes. "Last chance, boy. Red or green?"

I won't say "red" but I can't quite bring myself to say "green." Out loud, anyway. I mouth the word silently and Logan seems to understand it, because he shoves past me, still gripping my arm, then drags me through the living room, past the fireplace divider, and toward the dining room table. The other end, out of the way of the puzzle.

I stumble after him—these jeans are really tight and my dick is currently trying to drill through the fabric—and Logan shifts his hand from my arm to the back of my neck.

He pushes me up against the table, then exerts steady pressure on my neck until I'm bent over it. I brace my forearms on the tabletop. The table's edge is digging into my cock and Logan is a looming presence behind me. He bends over my back and growls in my ear, "Good boys get to come. Disrespectful boys get punished. Which are you?"

I wasn't trying to be disrespectful, but now that I'm on the verge of being punished for it, I'm so turned on I can't think. Holy fuck, how does he know every dirty fantasy I've ever had?

His large hand squeezes the back of my neck and he shakes me a little, like a dog with a toy in his mouth. "Well? Which is it?"

My mouth is suddenly dry and I swallow a few times, then lick my lips. "I, um, I don't think I'm a very good boy, Daddy."

He chuckles against my ear and goosebumps rise all over me. "No, you're not, are you?" He squeezes my neck once more, then lets go. "Stay," he orders.

I stay. Oh hells to the yes, I stay. Right where he put me.

He reaches underneath me and gets my jeans undone, then tugs them and my underwear down just far enough to expose my ass. My dick is still caught up in the front of my jeans and I'm probably going to end up with a button imprint on it.

And then Logan's hand comes down with a hard smack on my ass.

"Ugh," I grunt.

"Count, Silas," Logan says. "Out loud so I can hear you." He rubs his hand over the spot he spanked.

"One," I say, lifting my head from where it's been tucked between my arms.

His hand cracks down on my ass, hard enough to jostle me against the table. "Keep counting."

I fist my hands on the tabletop and gaze out the huge windows on the other side of the table. "Two," I grunt.

My skin heats up and my nipples go tight. My ass is on fire. Logan's got a hand like a shovel and I'm not sure how much more I can take. I keep counting, though my voice gets whispery and quiet because I can barely breathe. The heat is spreading through my whole body and my dick pulses every time Logan smacks my ass.

"I'm sorry, Daddy!" The yell bursts out of me just after Logan spanks me the fifth time. I don't even remember what I'm apologizing for, but it's enough, apparently, because he doesn't spank me again.

He squeezes my ass, first one cheek, then the other, and rubs the palm of his big hand all over my ass. It's soothing, but also ramps up my arousal. My dick is aching and I squirm a little against the table's edge.

Logan's got both his hands on my ass now, kneading and squeezing and rubbing my cheeks. And then he drags a chair toward him, sits down behind me, and kisses my smarting ass better. He spreads my cheeks and licks a long swath from my balls to my hole.

"I'm yours, Daddy." The words tumble from my mouth even as I cringe at how needy and desperate I sound. It's only for the weekend, Logan said so. Just to give me the revenge I came here for. It's not permanent.

"Please let me come, Daddy. I'll be good, I promise."

Logan swirls his tongue around my hole and my dick aches to be touched. I've fingered myself before, but I've never been rimmed, and oh my fucking God, it's amazing. The tip of his tongue wiggles at my hole and I'm desperate for him to enter me, but he pulls back.

"No." He exhales against my hot and aching skin and his breath is cool against my wet hole. "It's hardly a punishment if you come from it."

He stands up, and pushes the chair back with his foot. "Go drink that water, Silas. Don't make me tell you again."

I pull my jeans and underwear up over my blistered ass with some difficulty, then stumble to the kitchen and drink the freaking water. Logan comes into the kitchen, too, and bustles around, opening cabinets and drawers, getting ready to start making dinner.

"I'm gonna wash my face," I mutter at him, gesturing vaguely at the stairs. Logan nods.

"If you jerk off up there, I won't let you come for the rest of the night." Logan's deep voice floats up from the base of the stairs just as I get to his bathroom.

"Yes, Daddy," I call back. I think about jerking off anyway —I'm so turned on I can barely think about anything but how much I need to come—but I want to be good.

Well, I want to be bad too—that spanking was freaking *hot* —but I'm choosing to be good.

For now.

I splash cold water on my face until I've cooled down somewhat. Before I go back downstairs, I duck into Logan's bedroom and turn my back to the large mirror over his low dresser. I ease my jeans and underwear down over my ass, and look over my shoulder at the reflection.

My cheeks are mottled various shades of pink and white. There's a faint outline of overlapping handprints covering each cheek and my skin still feels hot to the touch, especially where the marks are darkest. No bruises and the marks are already starting to fade, but I like the contrast of the dark pink with the pale white of my skin.

It's evidence that someone wants me. Evidence that Logan put his hands on me and claimed me as something that belongs to him. And even if his claim won't last much longer than the marks will, at least I got to see it.

I pull my jeans up and manage to tuck my dick away without stroking it—which is a near thing—and button up. Then I head back downstairs to Logan.

Sixteen

LOGAN

I'M CUTTING RAW meat into chunks for dinner when Silas comes back downstairs and joins me in the kitchen, so I can't pull him toward me for a kiss. He perches gingerly on a stool on the other side of the island and props his chin in his hands.

"Can I do anything to help?" he asks.

"You can open that wine bottle," I say, jerking my chin at the Riesling on the counter. I generally prefer red wine over white, but this recipe calls for deglazing the pan with half a cup of white wine and it's a waste to not drink the rest.

Silas is familiar enough with the kitchen that he knows where I keep the wine key and the wine glasses. He opens the bottle with the efficiency of an experienced waiter and pours me a glass without being asked. He sets it near the cutting board where I'm slicing pork loin into chunks, but out of the way of stray raw meat juices.

"Thank you, sweetheart."

He smiles and resettles on the stool. He lets out a small hiss and stills, then shifts position, no doubt to accommodate his blistered ass.

"Feeling better after your spanking?"

His cheeks flush a dark pink and he ducks his head so his hair falls into his face. "Why was that so hot?" he mutters to the countertop.

"The pain gives you an endorphin rush," I tell him. "Endorphins are also released during sexual activity. For you, they're essentially the same."

"Do you like pain?"

"Not the way you do, baby. But I like hurting you." My skin tingles with the memory of watching my hand mark up his ass. I was hard the entire time I was spanking him, though I don't think he noticed, and my cock is still half-hard behind the prison of my pants. It'll keep, though.

"Isn't that kind of fucked up? You wanting to hurt me? I mean, would you still want to hurt me if you, like..." his throat works in a swallow. "Cared about me?" he finishes.

"I do care about you, baby." I shove down how very much I care about him. "But what else do you feel along with the pain? Can you tell me how you feel right now?"

"Well, my ass is freaking sore," he says, and I think he means to be snarky, but his tone is too languid to manage it.

"What else?" I insist. "What about the rest of you? Inside your head?"

He doesn't respond right away and I wait. I chop two chicken thighs into roughly bite-sized chunks before he answers.

"Quiet," he finally says. "Calm, I guess. Like I don't have to think about anything and I can let go and just be here."

"And that's what the pain gives you. The cage does it too, doesn't it?"

I look at him until he nods. "Giving up control. That's what you need, baby boy. That's what I like to give you."

"What about you?"

"What about me?"

"How do you get to this place in your head? Where it's all quiet and peaceful?"

I go to the sink to wash my hands, then come around the island and put my arms around him. He leans against me and I kiss the top of his head. "I get there by taking care of you, baby."

I don't want to give this boy up at the end of the weekend. The scent of my shampoo wafts up from Silas's hair. I hold him against me and breathe in. If there was any way I could keep him, I would.

For a single, breathless moment, I let myself imagine what it might be like to have Silas stay. To have him be the thing that changes everything, that turns my life upside down. A boy of my own—someone to take care of, but also someone I could fuck and love and punish.

It's not right, though. It can't last. At the end of the weekend, Silas will go back to the city and his job and a new life he'll create to be whatever he wants. He'll find someone closer to his own age. Hopefully someone who will understand what he needs and won't make him feel ashamed for it.

I'll go back to the way I was, too. To the life I've built for myself. Work that fills my days and most of my evenings and weekends, but that I genuinely enjoy. Dinners and galas and benefits that are not only client development but also keep me informed about new and emerging trends in the industry.

Hookups and one-night stands to slake my physical needs without getting emotionally entangled.

"Daddy?"

"Hmm?"

"I lo—" He stops and I can feel his throat move as he swallows. "I'm hungry."

And I'm back to where I am, where I can take care of Silas through this weekend, but that's all I can have. Christmas is next week and I'll eventually have to speak to my son again. I can't imagine that Silas will ever want to see him again, but I can't just cut Lance out of my life. Not even for Silas.

I kiss the top of Silas's head again and release him. "Let's finish making dinner, baby."

I put him to work peeling and chopping garlic cloves and a couple of carrots while I brown the chicken and pork. I allow him one glass of wine and we talk about inconsequential things, like the latest books we've read, and a film we both want to see.

Safe things.

I put a movie on after dinner and Silas curls up next to me on the sofa. I run my hand up and down his arm and knead the muscles of his shoulder, his back. He looks like he belongs here, in my home, wearing my shirt, his hair tousled from my fingers. I completely lose the plot of the movie, focusing instead on Silas.

Eventually, his head gets heavier in my lap and I think he's on the verge of falling asleep. "Bedtime, sweetheart."

He grumbles but sits up and rubs his knuckles into his eyes.

"Go upstairs and wash your face and brush your teeth," I tell him. "I'll be up in a few minutes."

By the time I turn out the lights, head upstairs, and finish brushing my own teeth, Silas is snuggled under the covers, just a spray of blond hair visible on the pillow. His clothes are draped over the chair by the windows, those bright Saxx boxer-briefs atop his dark jeans, so I know he's naked under there.

I take my own clothes off, tidy them away, and slip under the covers. Silas immediately turns into me, wrapping arms and legs around me like a spider monkey. "'Night, Daddy," he murmurs.

I kiss the top of his head. "Good night, baby boy."

I wake to Silas's mouth on my cock and a steady sucking that curls my toes and arches my back. When I open my eyes and reach down to wind my fingers in Silas's hair, he pulls off with a wet pop.

"Morning, Daddy," he says with a wide smile.

"Good morning, sweetheart." I've never seen Silas this chipper this early in the morning, but then again, this is only the second time he's woken in my bed. And after yesterday's nap and last night's early bedtime, he's probably more rested than usual.

And then I quit thinking about anything except Silas's mouth on my cock as he goes back down on me. I'm barely awake and his mouth is hot and wet, so I let him take control and I don't flip him over to fuck his throat the way I have so far.

He doesn't go easy on himself, though. His nose is buried in my pubes and my cock is nudging at the back of his throat. He stays there for an endless moment, throat working, cheeks hollowed, and it's glorious. I wish I could stay here forever and let Silas work me over until we both expire—him from asphyxiation and me from, I don't know, dehydration or starvation or something.

My hands are clenched in the sheets and I'm trying hard not to grab his head. He slides his hands under my hips, though, and squeezes. Which is all the encouragement I need. I dig my heels into the mattress, thrusting up enough to get that last infinitesimal inch down his throat.

Stars explode behind my eyes and my orgasm tears through me. Silas's throat milks me dry and I slump back on the bed. Silas licks my spent cock clean and sits up between my splayed thighs.

"Mmm," he says. He swipes the back of his hand across his mouth, looks at it, and licks a last couple of drops of come from it. "My favorite breakfast in bed."

"Not a very healthy breakfast," I say, but I'm too sated to chastise him.

He grins at me. "Not true. I Googled it once. There's a lot of protein in come. And it's got low calories."

"I don't think man can survive on come alone for very long," I say. He's adorable in his cheerfulness. His hair is sticking up six ways from Sunday and his cock is jutting out between his thighs. The balls of his ladder piercings create a double rainbow on the underside of his shaft.

It's the prettiest thing I've seen in a long time.

"Stroke yourself," I tell him. "Show me how you get yourself off."

He doesn't need convincing, my eager boy, and takes himself in hand. His fingers are long and slim, the nails cut short but painted the same rainbow of colors as the beads in his piercings. The paint is chipped on a few nails and I make a mental note to schedule a manicure appointment for him tomorrow.

Until I remember that today is our last day together. And that I'm not responsible for taking care of him after today.

I put that thought aside. No use worrying about tomorrow when I've got this beautiful boy on his knees before me now, stroking his beautiful cock, looking at me with his beautiful eyes, shining with lust.

He starts slow, dragging his hand from root to tip. He cups himself underneath so that his palm rubs the ladder bars under the skin and his fingertips and thumb barely skim along the top of his shaft. Until he reaches the head and his fingers and thumb come together to circle it and bump over the glans.

I stack the pillows behind my head, propping myself up for a better view. He spreads his knees, sinks a little more onto his heels, and takes his time stroking himself.

His breath is coming a little faster now and he slides his other hand up his body to pinch a nipple. I want to touch him. I want to push him onto his back, knock his hands away and take control of his pleasure. I tuck my hands under my head to keep from doing it.

I asked for this. I told him to get himself off so I could watch. The small ache of denying the control I want to take is worth it.

Silas is still watching me. His strokes are faster now and his fingers are plucking at and twisting his nipple ring.

"That's it, pretty boy. Show your Daddy how you like to be touched."

Seventeen

SILAS

OH GOD. LOGAN'S words do more to me than my own hand on my dick. When he looks at me like he is now, I feel pretty. Not just hot because I'm naked and I've got my dick in my hand and who doesn't get a little turned on when they're looking at a guy stroking himself?

These last few months, the only way I could get Lance to have sex was to be naked when he came to bed and already hard. He'd let me suck him and stay awake long enough for me to jerk myself off, though he quit touching my dick when I got the piercings, even after they healed and I told him he could.

But with Logan, I feel seen. Like he sees all of me—the parts I show to the world and the parts I'm afraid to show—and he actually likes everything. I love that.

I almost told him that I love him. Last night, after he spanked me. When I felt so quiet and peaceful that I nearly lost the filter between my brain and my mouth. But I caught myself just in time and I don't think Logan noticed.

Although there's little he doesn't notice. He noticed right away that I like it when sex hurts a little. Lance never noticed that. How can I have had sex for two years with a person who never bothered to notice—or ask—what I like?

"Silas." Logan's voice brings me back and I remember that I'm supposed to be putting on a show for my Daddy. "Let me see you come, baby boy."

I get back to stroking myself and the closer I get, the softer Logan's face goes. His eyes flick from my dick to my nipples to my face. He's watching how I touch myself, yeah, but he's also looking at me. How each stroke or tug on my nipples affects me. Like he's not so much cataloging what motions I like—though I bet he's doing that too—but really reveling in my pleasure for my sake.

And so I quit thinking about this as an exhibition and just sink into the way it feels. I focus on the sparks of electricity zinging through my nerves at each twist of a nipple ring, the slick friction when the head of my dick slides through the tight circle of my fingers, the heat coiling at the base of my spine, and my Daddy looking at me like I'm the prettiest thing he's ever seen.

I think it's his smile that does me in. A small one, just a tiny lift of the corners of his lips. He's got answering crinkles at the corners of his eyes, and I recognize this is his private smile, meant just for me.

I tip over the cliff and shudder as my dick jerks and empties all over his chest and groin. My heart is pounding and I feel light-headed. Daddy sits up before I'm even finished and wraps his arms around me, holding me upright and close to him.

"That's it, sweetheart." He's murmuring other things in my ear and I don't catch all of it because I'm still shaking and panting and my pulse is pounding in my temples. I close my eyes and rest my forehead on his chest.

When I recover and open my eyes, there's come smeared all over both of us. It's drying in Logan's chest hair and my hand is sticky. I peel myself away and settle back on my heels.

"Shower?" Logan suggests with that same tiny smile.

"Yeah," I say.

Since we both just got off, the shower's mostly about getting us clean. Logan washes me, though, and all I have to do is stand there and let him move me around. I almost get hard again when he washes my hair, because his fingers dig into my scalp like a deep-tissue massage.

And then he slides a soap-slick finger between my ass cheeks. That gets me hard, for sure, though I dunno if I can come again so soon. Logan scrubs around my hole and presses gently against it.

"You'll wear the plug again this morning, and later, we'll work up to you taking my cock."

"Yes, Daddy," I manage. *Finally*. I've been waiting what seems like forever for Logan to fuck me. My stomach erupts into butterflies at the thought that he'll finally do it.

And then I remember what else he bought with the plug. "What about the cage?"

Logan grasps my dick and I can't help thrusting in the soapy circle of his fingers. "How will you fit in that cage with an erection like this, boy?"

I thought I was sated, but if he keeps this up—fingering my hole while stroking me maddeningly slowly—I'm going to come again soon. "It's your fault, Daddy," I manage, my panting breath fogging up the shower stall.

Logan chuckles behind me and withdraws his hands. "You're absolutely right, Silas."

I look over my shoulder, but he's already stepping out of the shower. "Hey! I didn't mean you should stop."

"It's time for good boys to have breakfast. A proper breakfast."

Logan dries himself off and holds a towel out for me. I grumble, but I make sure it's under my breath so he pretends to ignore me. He dries me off and I try to think of things that aren't sexy to get my dick to go down. Nothing works until I remember walking in on Lance getting face-fucked in a darkened office.

Yep, that'll do it.

"Stay there," Logan says. He disappears for a minute into his bedroom and I stare at myself in the mirror while I brush my teeth. You know what? I'm tired of thinking about Lance. I'm tired of comparing him to Logan. It's inevitable, since Logan is Lance's father and that's the whole reason I came here in the first place—to get revenge on Lance by fucking his dad.

But it's turning into more than that.

I think.

Ugh, it's so confusing. Maybe I shouldn't have started down this road in the first place. I probably should have given myself time to get over Lance. Maybe find someone new in a few months.

But then I see Logan coming up behind me in the mirror. He's put on a pair of lounge pants but he's still shirtless and he's got the plug in one hand and a bottle of lube in the other, the cage hooked around a finger of the hand holding the plug.

I don't want to find someone new in a few months. I don't want to try to meet someone in a crowded club where the music's too loud to even hear their name. I don't want to sift through a bunch of randos on a dating app and waste time getting to know someone only to find out that we're not compatible.

Logan and I already know each other. Okay, not in the biblical sense until this weekend, but I've always liked spending time with him. Just doing the jigsaw puzzle with him yesterday and talking about my musical during breakfast was almost as nice as the sex we've been having.

At least for me. I hope Logan enjoyed it too. It was his idea to spend the weekend together, after all. But that's when it ends, right? I mean, he can't really want to spend more time with a kid my age.

Can he?

"Step back a bit, baby." I take a step back from the sink and Logan's arms come around me from behind. His chest is warm against my back. He sets the plug on the edge of the sink and squirts a small dollop of lube on his fingers. He smears the lube over the head of my dick and gets everything tucked into the cage before I get too hard.

It's a little like the aftermath of being spanked, without the heat and pain first. I can feel my mind settling. There's nothing I need to do or worry about now, because Daddy's in charge of everything now.

What I do, when I get hard, when I come.

If I get to come.

I sort of slump back against him and he strokes his hands up my stomach and chest and hugs me tight against him. "There. Look at my pretty boy now."

I look at us in the mirror. My hair is wet and hanging in clumps around my face. My skin is still flushed from the shower we just took and I'm not wearing any eye makeup or lip gloss. I look incredibly young, especially compared to Logan's silver hair and the handful of lines on his face.

But he's got that little smile on his face again. And I look happy. Happier than I've felt in months.

Logan reaches for the lube again. "Spread your legs and bend over, sweetheart."

Words that would be guaranteed to get me hard, if I wasn't caged. Which I guess explains why he put the cage on me first.

I do as he says and the lube and the metal plug are cool against my hole. I exhale as he pushes the plug slowly inside me. A wave of heat rushes through my body. I cannot wait for him to fuck me.

"I can't wait to fuck you, baby boy." It's like Logan heard my thoughts, echoing them back at me. He spreads my cheeks apart and taps the ring of the plug so that it jostles inside me. It lights my nerve endings up and I go up on my toes a little.

Then he strokes a hand over my ass cheek and I tense a little in anticipation. If he spanks me, I am going to come, regardless of the cage.

He doesn't, though. One more caress and he says, "Breakfast first. Put some clothes on and come downstairs."

He leaves and I splash some water on my face to cool down. I put on the clothes Logan left for me on the dresser—my jeans and another of his long-sleeved wool shirts. Guess I should have brought some clothes with me. But how was I to know I'd end up spending the entire weekend here?

If I'm honest, I mostly expected Logan to pat me on the shoulder and send me home. Sure, there's always been this spark between us, but I hadn't really expected him to act on it.

I glance at the big bed in the middle of the room, which Logan made at some point when I was in the bathroom. It still feels a little weird to be in his bedroom, especially alone. Everything about it is just so...Logan.

It's neat as a pin and organized like everything else in his house. Feeling a little like an intruder and a little like a stalkery serial killer looking for a trophy, I peek in his big, walk-in closet. There's a line of business suits hanging on thick wooden hangers, mostly black, charcoal gray, or navy blue, but there are a couple of tan suits and a blue and cream seersucker that I saw him in when Lance brought me to some cousin's wedding last year.

His dress shirts hang on an upper rod. There are a lot of white shirts but also pink and pale blue and lavender, some with pinstripes and checks. The rack of ties hanging next to the shirts is an explosion of colors and patterns. I run my hand along them and the silk slips through my fingers like water.

And now instead of imagining I'm a serial killer choosing a trophy, I'm imagining Logan dressed for work, in one of the charcoal suits, standing next to a big mahogany desk, looking at me with that little smile on his face. He loosens his tie— maybe this blue one with the tiny white flowers on it—and I brush the silk along the inside of my wrist. Maybe he'd tie my hands together with it.

Heat pools at the base of my dick, but there's nowhere for it to go. The thudding pressure of blood stalled because of the cage makes me feel lightheaded and floaty.

"Silas!" Logan calls from downstairs and I remember where I'm supposed to be.

Eighteen

LOGAN

SILAS IS A little flushed when he gets downstairs, but settles on what I'm now starting to think of as his stool at the kitchen island, and takes the cup of coffee I hand him with a sweet smile. I slice some mushrooms, dice a bell pepper and half an onion, and chop a couple of tomatoes for an omelette. He scarfs it down with gratifying speed.

Damn, it's good to watch my boy eating the breakfast I made for him. Even if Silas is only my boy for the weekend. We still have the rest of the day together.

I'm trying to decide when to bring up his post-Lance plans and how I can help when I notice that he's staring out the sliding glass door that leads out to the patio.

"What are you thinking about, sweetheart?"

Silas swivels his head around to look at me like he's been caught doing something naughty. He's been tapping his fingers lightly on the table next to his plate, and his hand darts into his lap.

"Oh, um. Sorry, I was just..." He hums something under his breath and then shakes his head like he's dislodging something in his brain. "I just had an idea for one of the songs in Act Two. I don't want to lose it, is all."

"Write it down, then," I suggest.

"Wish I had my laptop," he mutters under his breath as he pushes back from the table to find his phone. "Or my keyboard."

"Use the piano downstairs." The lower level of my house is a large space with an entertainment center, some workout equipment for when I'm here and don't have access to my regular gym, and a baby grand piano that I bought years ago when Lance briefly took piano lessons. Silas is the only one who's played it in ages.

He pauses at the kitchen doorway. "But we're supposed to be..." He blushes a delightful pink. I love his mixture of shyness and enthusiastic filthiness.

"We've got the whole day ahead of us, baby. If you want to work on your musical for a while, you should."

"You don't mind? I mean, I want to be with you. I just can't get this bit out of my head." He hums a few bars of something that sounds hauntingly melodic. "See, I've been using C major for Jocasta's lament, but if I change it to A minor, it might sound better. A little darker, but still hopeful, you know?"

I know very little about music composition, but I nod. "Go on, then, sweetheart. Do you want to take the plug out or the cage off while you're working?"

Silas casts a glance down at his crotch. "Oh. Um, no, it's okay." He looks back at me with a sly expression. "A reminder not to get too distracted from you, Daddy."

I get up from the table and cross the kitchen to kiss him. "That's my dirty boy."

He kisses back with such enthusiasm that I consider re-thinking the plan we just made for the morning and dragging him back to bed. He tastes like coffee and smells like my sham-poo. I'm struck with how much I want this with him. Kisses after breakfast, making plans together to do our respective work, more kisses.

I want this every morning. With Silas.

He's squirming in my arms now, rubbing his chest against mine. I worm a hand between us and press the heel of my palm against his nipple. He twists his torso, dragging his nipple ring across my hand. He pants into my mouth and I nip at his bottom lip.

"You have work to do, baby," I remind him when I can finally pull back from his lips.

"I can do it later," he says. He sways toward me, his lips shiny and wet, his eyes half-closed, just a sliver of green behind the dark honey of his long eyelashes. "I don't even remember what I was going to do."

"All the more reason to get it done now." I let him go but not before squeezing his nipple between my fingers for a long moment. He arches his back and tips his chin up enough that I can see his throat work as he swallows. "You wanted to get it down before you lose the idea, right?"

"Yeah, but..."

"Are you arguing with me, Silas?"

He opens his eyes and looks at me. "Oh. Um, no, Daddy."

I chuck him under the chin. "There's a good boy." I'd kiss him again, but it's too easy to get lost in kissing him. "Go on, then."

He turns and leaves the kitchen without further argument. I head upstairs to my study. I have plenty of work I can do while Silas is composing, but there are a few things I want to take care of first.

I've barely started when I realize that I need some information, so I go back downstairs to the hook where Silas's coat hangs. I feel a twinge of guilt as I dig in the pockets for his wallet. It's for his own good, though. I'll tell him why later, but I'm not asking permission for this.

Even if he doesn't stay my boy, he needs someone to take care of him.

I jot down the information from his driver's license, and score—his social security card is tucked behind his Dramatists Guild card. Excellent. I write the number down and put his wallet back where I found it.

I leave my study door open so I can faintly hear Silas noodling around on the piano downstairs. There's a short melodic phrase he keeps returning to—the motif of the song he's writing, I presume—and I can hear how it sounds slightly different as he plays it different ways. Different keys, I suppose, like he said.

He seems to settle on one version and plays the melody over a series of chords, then starts from what sounds like might be the beginning of the song. He's singing along but I can't make out the words. It sounds like what he said, though—sad and filled with longing, but also hopeful at the end.

While Silas is working, I finish the tasks I've set for myself. Bank account opened, in Silas's name, but linked to mine. First deposit made, ten grand to start, and recurring deposits set up.

I place a call to a real estate agent who's married to a client and give her a heads up about what I think we'll be looking for. I'll leave it to Silas to choose what we go see, of course.

It doesn't take long to make these arrangements and Silas is still playing piano, so I settle in to do some work. James Cohen hasn't gotten back to me yet, but it's still early. I've known him long enough to know that he sleeps late on Sundays and has a long, usually boozy, brunch with his husband. I don't expect to hear from him until mid-afternoon at the earliest.

I pull up a standard production contract and start putting in some basic information, but that feels a little like tempting fate so I turn to some work for my actual clients instead.

I'm halfway through marking up the offering documents for a play a client is considering investing in—that I'm fairly certain is going to flop six weeks from opening night, despite the promising regional performances—when I realize Silas has stopped playing.

I wait another five minutes to see if he'll start again and then close my laptop. When I reach the lower level, Silas is bent over the music rack at the piano.

He's scribbling on some blank music manuscript paper. Well, not blank anymore, since there are notes in his precise handwriting covering half or more of the page.

I linger in the doorway. I don't want to disrupt his concentration. And he's beautiful when he's working, so I don't mind just watching him for a while. The tip of his tongue is sticking out a bit between his lips and the long fingers on his left hand tap out a rhythm on the piano's lid before his other hand writes it out on the manuscript paper.

He runs his hand through his hair and sticks the pencil behind his ear, then hums a variation of the melody he's been working on under his breath. He scribbles more notes on the paper, then props it up on the music rack and sets the pencil aside.

He opens and closes both hands, flexes his fingers, and plays the piece from start to finish. It's lovely. The low chords underlying the song are dark and the lyrics express such sadness and longing, but the chorus is simple enough that I find myself humming along at its next round.

Which is when he looks up and catches sight of me in the doorway. He smiles, then sings the last lines as he finishes playing what he's written.

"That's wonderful, sweetheart."

His cheeks turn pink and he runs his fingers over the keyboard, repeating the final chords of the song. "You think so?"

"I do. There won't be a dry eye in the house."

He snorts. "Yeah, if I can ever finish it and find someone to produce it."

"You will," I tell him. James Cohen is first on my list, but he's not the only producer I know.

Silas ducks his head and his hair falls into his face. I come up behind him at the piano and stroke his head. His hair is silky and baby-fine, the strands slipping through my fingers like water.

"It's just hard, you know?" he says. He's looking at his fingers, twisting and flexing in his lap. "Living with Lance helped, because I didn't have to pay rent. I mean, I like my job, actually—it's great for people-watching and the tips are usually excellent."

Silas works for a catering company that does high-end events. Not the one my firm hired for its party, thank Christ. I don't know what he'd have done if the guy blowing my asshole son had been a colleague.

"But I'm gonna have to work more events now and that's less time to write and there just aren't enough hours in the day, you know?"

"I know, baby," I say softly. I shift so that I can massage his shoulders, digging my fingers into the muscles over his shoulder blades, working out the tension there. "I'll—"

"I'm not asking for help," he says suddenly. "I'll be fine, really. I'm just...bitching for no reason, I guess."

No reason except losing his boyfriend and the place he was living, all at once. Damn Lance for doing this to him. Except that if he hadn't, Silas wouldn't be here with me right now.

I hold off on telling him about the arrangements I've just made. Later. When he's not thinking about his ex-boyfriend. When I can figure out a way of explaining how honored and happy helping him would make me. Without damaging his pride or suggesting he can't take care of himself.

I know he can. I just don't want him to have to.

"That feels nice," Silas murmurs. I'm still massaging his shoulders and I press my thumbs on either side of the channel of his spine and drag them firmly down to just about his waistband. Silas groans just like when I suck him and it goes straight to my cock.

I pull him upright so his back is against my chest. He tips his head back and looks up at me. I smooth the hair back from his forehead. "Silas," I say. "You've got your whole life ahead of you. There's plenty of time to achieve your dreams."

His lips purse and he blows a puff of air. "Is that your way of telling me I'm just a kid?"

"Is that what I said?"

Another puff of air and he blinks those green eyes. "No," he concedes. "But..."

"But what?"

Silas shrugs, which causes his back to rub against the hard line of my erection. I shuffle closer to him and my cock slots along the channel of his spine. "Does that feel like I think of you as a kid?"

"No." His heartbeat picks up and he squirms on the hard seat of the piano bench.

Nineteen

SILAS

I'D MANAGED TO forget about the cock cage and the plug in my ass while I was working, but now I can't think of anything else. Except Logan's hard dick pressing against my spine and his arms wrapped around me, holding me tight.

I seriously don't know why Logan puts up with me. Who comes to seduce a man like him and then spends most of the time *not* fucking? I mean, yesterday, I slept half the afternoon. This morning, Logan promised to fuck me—something I've wanted since the day I met him, even if I didn't recognize it at the time—and now it's almost noon and I've just been dicking around on his piano instead of letting him dick me down.

And to top it off, I keep bitching about Lance. Who wants to fuck someone who can't keep another man out of their head?

And okay, it's not Lance himself I keep thinking about, but what I'm going to do now that Lance and I broke up. But none of that is Logan's problem and if I keep being a buzzkill about where I'm going to live and how I'm going to have to get a real job to pay rent and whatever, then I should go and deal with my problems instead of taking up his weekend.

"Whatever you're thinking about can wait." It's Logan's Daddy voice. The one that shuts up the constant stream of anxious thoughts running through my brain.

I let my head fall back against his chest and close my eyes. He wraps one hand around my throat. "Look at me, Silas."

I open my eyes and look up at him. He's staring down at me, his hazel eyes serious, his lips in a firm line.

"You agreed to do what I tell you, yes?"

I can't nod with Logan's hand squeezing my throat. I can barely speak, but I manage a whisper. "Yes, Daddy."

"And I'm telling you that now is not the time to worry about your future. I will help you figure out what you're going to do next, but for now, all you have to do is be here with me. Can you do that?"

"Yes, Daddy."

"Do I need to spank you to quiet your thoughts?"

Jesus, if he spanks me now, I'm going to come immediately, despite the cage. "No, Daddy," I whisper. "Not right now."

"Okay." He squeezes my throat a little harder and holy shit, all the blood in my body rushes south but can't fill my dick. Spots dance before my eyes and I'd fall off this bench into a puddle on the ground if Logan wasn't holding me up.

By my throat. Restricting my breathing. It's working, though. I can't think about anything else but him. And whether he'll let me go. God, I don't want him to.

He does, of course. The tight vise of his fingers loosens slowly, incrementally, like he doesn't want to let go, either. He tips my chin up and bends to give me an upside-down kiss.

"Go upstairs," he murmurs against my lips. "Get undressed and lie on your back on the bed."

The bed. Not *his* bed. Almost like it's our bed.

"Yes, Daddy." I have to cough to clear my throat and I can still feel the phantom squeeze of his hand around it.

Logan steps back so I can swing my legs around the piano bench and stand up. I sway a little when I do, still lightheaded from him choking me. He reaches out to steady me.

I reach to clear my manuscript paper and shit from the piano, but Logan nudges me toward the door. "Leave it. It'll be here when we're done."

I drift toward the stairs, still in the mindless daze that letting Daddy take control puts me in, and it's not until I reach the top that I realize Logan isn't behind me. I hear the door to the garage open but I've been given very simple instructions and all I have to do is obey them.

I strip my clothes off, fold them as neat as I can, and lie down on the bed. It's not long until Logan appears in the bedroom doorway, a tangle of some sort of thin rope in one hand. *Oh.*

Oh, hell yes.

He doesn't tie me up immediately, though. He takes his own clothes off and kneels up on the bed. I spread my legs and he shifts up in between them. His hands are firm and warm when they settle on the inside of my thighs, bracketing my caged cock.

"So pretty for me, baby," he murmurs. He bends and licks at the skin squeezed between the concentric rings and oh my god, the contrast of his warm, wet tongue and the hard metal containing me is gonna make me lose my mind.

My fists are clenching in the sheets and I'm sliding my heels along them, scrambling for purchase, lifting my hips, desperate for more. He tucks his hand under my caged balls and I look down my body at the cage resting in the palm of his hand.

Jesus, I look so *small* in his big hand. My dick is turning pinker by the second and the thudding pulse at my groin is echoing in my ears and dragging me into a place where nothing matters but Logan touching me.

"I was going to tie you up, but I think I like watching you squirm."

"Daddy, *please.*"

"Please what?"

I don't know what. I want him to tie me up but I want to be free to roll around on his bed with abandon. I want to come and I want this anticipation of coming to last forever. I want him to fuck me and I want to stay his boy as long as he'll have me.

"*Please,*" I moan again, trusting that he'll decide for me and that whatever he decides is what I need.

"I've got you, baby," he says. He straightens up and stretches over me, a long arm reaching for the nightstand. His chest hovers briefly over my face and I dart my tongue out and lick his nipple. Even as lost in sensation as I am, I want to make Logan feel as good as he makes me feel. His nipple tightens and he stays in place long enough for me to suck it into a hard point.

He pulls back, though, and resettles between my legs. He spreads my thighs wide, bends my legs, and pushes my knees toward my chest. "Hold yourself open for me, sweetheart."

I catch behind my knees and pull my legs in. Logan's fingers slip along the creases where my thighs meet my groin and there's a brief tug on my balls and then the cage is off and my dick springs straight up like a rocket. "Oh, fuck," I moan. A bead of pre-come wells up at my slit and drips down my shaft.

Logan sits back on his heels. He sets the cage off somewhere to the side and then slides his hands up and down my thighs. It's like he knows that if he touches my dick, it'll be all over.

He leans over me again, reaching for the lube in the night-stand drawer. This time, I'm concentrating too much on not coming to lick at his nipple, but he doesn't seem to mind. When he settles again in between my thighs, he reaches for the plug still inside me.

He draws it out halfway—ever so slowly—until the widest part is stretching me open, and stops there.

"I can't wait to be inside you, baby boy."

I can't wait, either. I whimper as he pushes the plug back in. He pumps it in and out a few more times and I pull my legs higher and tighter. "Fuck me, Daddy. *Please.*"

He chuckles and draws the plug out again. This time, it pops all the way out and I'm suddenly empty and bereft.

"Shhh," Daddy whispers. "I'm right here, baby."

Thick fingers nudge at my hole—two of them, I think. He presses them in slowly and I hear myself moan so loud the neighbors are gonna hear. I've used my own fingers before, but the angle's awkward that way, and Logan's fingers are bigger than mine. Longer, too. He brushes against a spot inside me that makes my vision short out and my hips jerk.

I can't hold out anymore. I bend nearly in half when I come and I think it splashes onto my own chin, but Logan is still thrusting his fingers in and out of my hole and I'm making noises I can barely hear while my orgasm tears through me.

I'm still shivering from the aftershocks when Logan pulls his fingers free and tugs me upright and wraps his arm around me. I slump against his chest but he doesn't cuddle me, just bends me over my own knees so I'm face down on the bed, my ass propped up on my heels. He swings a leg over me and spreads my cheeks open with both hands.

There's a blunt, latex-covered, pressure against my hole. It increases, hard and unyielding, until I'm not sure I can take anymore, and then eases.

"Push back against me, baby." Logan's voice is strained. The pressure of his dick returns, slick and hot, and I do like he says. Or I try anyway, and I can feel his thumbs spreading me as open as I can go.

It's not enough, though. He's too big. I can feel him against me and it's hot and sharp and I think there's absolutely no way he's going to fit, when something shifts and he slides just a bit inside.

"That's my boy," he croons behind me. There's a cool stroke of something slick around the edges of my hole. "Take me, take your Daddy like I know you can, baby boy."

More aching, hard pressure and I think I might split in two. I groan into the mattress and push back against him again. He slides another inch or so inside and this time he keeps going. He presses forward like nothing is going to stop him.

I'm certainly not. It hurts. There's a sharp pinch at my entrance and a burning pressure inside where he's grinding deeper into me.

I love it.

When he's finally all the way inside, he bends over me and tucks his face into where my neck meets my shoulder. "Good boy," he breathes next to my ear. "You're such a good boy for me."

I am impaled on him and he surrounds me, his chest a hot, heavy weight against my back, his arms bracketing mine. He slides his hands down my forearms and tangles our fingers together. My hole is stretched wide and every breath he takes twitches his cock inside me a tiny bit. If I could stay like this forever, I would.

Logan sucks a hard kiss on my neck and then he's no longer blanketing me. He peels himself off my back and hooks his fingers around my hips. "I'm going to fuck you until your hole is red and swollen, baby boy. All you need to do is let me."

I stand corrected. That is what I want forever. Logan's cock sawing in and out of me while I lay still and let him. I breathe out and my whole body relaxes, which lets Logan slide that last tiny bit into me.

"Yes," he groans. He pulls out slowly and that makes me groan, too. It still burns when he moves inside me, and before I can adjust, Logan shoves back into me.

Twenty

SILAS

LOGAN SETS UP A STEADY PACE, thrusting into me over and over, ignoring my grunts, indifferent to whether I'm really open enough for this.

It's the indifference that really does it for me.

"Oh, fuck. Your cock is so big, Daddy," I moan. "I love how big you are."

I'm getting close—again—and I'm not even touching my dick. Again. Logan's got his hands on my hips, fingers drilling into the thin skin over my hip bones, so he's not touching me, either. I'm going to have bruises there later, I'm pretty sure, and I don't care.

Logan jerks my hips back against him, slamming his cock into me. Its thick, hard length drags over my prostate, causing sparks of electricity to shoot all through my body. I'm so fucking close and I think my heart might stop when I come, but what a way to go.

"Daddy," I groan. Logan grips me harder at my hips. There's a sound outside the bedroom that doesn't register at first.

The slam of a heavy door. A voice calling from the bottom of the stairs.

I push back against the thick cock that's filling me, stretching me wide, and scraping over and over that spot inside. Lightning flickers through my nerves and I'm so close that I'm desperate for it, a string of moans and nonsense falling from my panting mouth, all around the word that spirals me higher each time I say it.

Daddy.

And that's when my ex appears in Logan's bedroom doorway.

"Hey, Dad, I'm…"

Logan didn't shut his bedroom door when we came upstairs, so Lance is suddenly just right there. While his father's cock is in my ass, my own dick leaking and about to explode all over his father's bed. I don't know whether Logan sees Lance until he wrestles me upright so my back is pressed against him and his arm is an iron bar across my chest. He's stopped moving inside me, but he doesn't pull out. Instead, he grasps my dick in his other hand and jacks me with short, brutal strokes.

"Come for me, baby boy," he growls in my ear, low enough that I don't think Lance can hear him.

And I do.

I arch against him and stare into Lance's shocked face while my dick spurts ropes of white across the rumpled bedspread. My vision goes a little hazy at the edges but I keep my eyes open and staring at my ex-boyfriend. While his father strokes my dick until it softens.

Only then does Logan say, "Get out, Lance."

Lance's jaw is slack and his eyes are like saucers. "What the…" he starts. "You're…I mean, what the…"

"Get out!" Logan roars. He's still got his arm around me, bracing me against his chest, and his hand is loosely holding my now soft, damp cock.

Lance spins on his heel and disappears. I hear his footsteps head down the stairs.

"Oh my god," I say. I don't know what else to say. I came here for exactly this reason—to get revenge on Lance for cheating on me by fucking his dad—but now that Lance actually witnessed said revenge, I'm not sure how I feel.

Not triumphant, really. Or superior, or anything like that. Mostly kind of numb, as it turns out.

Logan kisses the side of my head and slowly, gently pulls out of me. Way more gently than he'd shoved into me. "I'll talk to him," he says while he's pulling the condom off.

I shake my head. I'm still on my knees, kind of folded over myself without Logan holding me up, but I push myself upright with shaking arms. "No, I'll do it."

"Silas," Logan starts. His voice has that fatherly concern that sends shivers down my spine, but this is a problem of my own making and I gotta deal with it.

"I'll talk to him," I say, and this time, Logan doesn't argue.

I pull my jeans on. This wasn't the way I'd planned to have it out with Lance, but I'm a big boy, despite Logan calling me his baby. I can sack up and deal with my ex.

Even if I have to do it while my hole is aching from his father fucking me and lube is slipping stickily between my ass cheeks.

Lance is standing in the middle of his childhood bedroom, looking around at the furnishings like he's never seen them before. He crosses his arms across his chest when he sees me hovering in the doorway.

"So, what? Does this make us even now?"

"Even?" I thought I'd feel a twinge of guilt about fucking his dad, but screw that. "What the fuck is that supposed to mean?" "You caught me getting a blow job from someone else so I gotta catch you fucking my dad?" "The difference is that you cheated on me, Lance! How many others have there been that I don't even know about?"

He has the decency to look a little ashamed, at least. "Look, I know, okay, and I shouldn't have done that. But you just fucked my *dad*, Silas."

"Yeah, I did." I pull my shoulders back and tuck my thumbs into the belt loops of my jeans. As usual, Lance's eyes skitter away from my chest and my nipple piercings and rest somewhere over my shoulder. "He's *my* Daddy now," I say. And okay, I do feel a twinge of vindication when he flinches at that.

"For fuck's sake, Silas, that's disgusting."

"Your dad doesn't seem to think so. At least he isn't a cheating asshole."

"My dad hasn't had a relationship longer than one night in my entire life, so how the hell would you know that?" Lance narrows his eyes at me. "Wait, how long has this been going on?" Oh, fuck him sideways. "Once again, I'm not the one who cheated! When the hell would I have even found time for that?" Between waiting tables, working my ass off to get my play produced, and trying to make our relationship work, I barely have two moments to string together.

He looks at me. At my face, for a change, for what feels like the first time in months. Then he sighs and his puffed-up indignation deflates. "Yeah, I know. You wouldn't do that."

Damn right, I wouldn't. Even if I'd been secretly wanting to for years. Lance doesn't need to know that, though. Even after everything he's done, I don't need to hurt him like that.

"For what it's worth, I am sorry, Silas," Lance says. "I don't know how shit got all fucked up between us."

Now it's my turn to sigh. "It hasn't been working for a while. We probably should have broken up months ago."

He nods. "Probably. That guy doesn't mean anything to me. I don't even know why I did it. I guess I just..." He stops and darts his eyes guiltily away from mine.

"Needed a quick way to dump me? Other than, you know, talking to me?" I'm still fucking pissed and he flinches.

He takes a step toward me and I take one step back. "I'm really sorry, Silas. I should have talked to you. I should have just ended it clean."

"No shit," I say, but he sounds sincere and the apology soothes a bit of my hurt. I think he might actually mean it. I mean, he's a cheating douchebag, and he can sometimes be insensitive as fuck, but he's almost never intentionally cruel. And he is capable of taking responsibility for his actions, apparently.

There's a beat of silence between us, long enough that we can hear Logan moving around in his bedroom above us. Lance glances up at the ceiling. "I can't believe you let my dad fuck you."

"He's gonna let me fuck him in return," I say, because I'm a little shit and I can't help myself. I don't actually know whether that's true or not—Logan might not be vers and I might not like doing the fucking as much as being fucked, but it's worth it for the cringe expression on Lance's face.

"Jesus, Silas," he says. He covers his eyes with his hand as if blocking out the sight. "You know what? I'm just gonna pretend you didn't say that."

He hesitates and then asks, "Is this just for tonight, or are you...?"

I cross my own arms over my chest and just stare at him. It's a fair question, I guess. Logan's his dad and Christmas is next week, and if Lance is wondering whether he'll walk in on the same scene on Christmas Eve... You know what? I'm not inclined to reassure him on this point, even after his apology. But also, I have no freaking idea what happens between me and Logan after this weekend.

"Never mind," Lance says. There's another awkward silence and then he runs a hand through his hair and gestures vaguely around him. "I actually came up to ask Dad if he would let you stay here while you figure out what you want to do. I know you've been staying at Chloe's and she's got all those roommates, so it's gotta be crowded."

That's an understatement.

"And even if you're pissed at me," Lance continues. "And I deserve it," he says hastily at my look. "Dad's got all this space and you could still get back and forth to work on the train. And you know that whatever happens between us, Dad would take care of you."

I cock a brow at him and he claps a hand over his mouth. "Oh my god, that is *not* what I meant, Silas."

I just keep looking at him, and he's looking back at me, and then his mouth twitches and so does mine, and we both bust out laughing. He bends over double and I slump to the floor and we're cackling like loons. I'm surprised Logan hasn't come to find out what on earth we could be laughing at under the circumstances.

Finally, I calm down and wipe tears from my eyes. Lance's guffaws trail off to intermittent giggles. It's actually a nice thought Lance had—to acknowledge that my relationship with his dad is a separate thing from the relationship we had—and to care enough about me to make sure I have a place to stay. Even if he's the goddamn reason I have to move out of the place I thought I had.

"Yeah, well, I'll come get the rest of my shit sometime next week." I don't know where I'll put it, but Lance is right. Logan would probably let me keep it here for a while.

He nods. "Give me a heads up and I'll be there to help. Or not be there, whichever you prefer."

"Yeah," I say. "Okay."

We stand there for a few minutes, just looking at each other, and there's really nothing else to say. Lance runs his hand through his hair and then says, "Okay. Well, I guess I'll see you around, Silas."

"Yeah."

"Take care of yourself."

I give him a smirk and he holds a hand up. "Nope, not gonna go there, dude. Don't even."

I'm beyond ready for him to leave, so I don't make any cracks about who will be taking care of whom if I stay with his dad like he suggested. "See you around, Lance."

I step out of his way so he can leave. He doesn't say goodbye to his dad, which, under the circumstances, I get.

Logan has left us to our own devices and I know he's gotta be wondering what the hell went down, but I take a minute to flop face-first down on Lance's bed.

What the fuck am I gonna do now?

Twenty-One

LOGAN

IT'S KILLING ME to leave the boys alone. To leave Silas with the man who hurt him so much. To not storm into Lance's room and demand to know what the fuck he's doing here. To rail at him that I'd raised him better than to cheat on someone and betray their trust like he'd done to Silas.

But it's Silas's hurt and not mine, and if he's going to find any closure with Lance, he's not going to find it with me hovering over them like a...well, like a *dad*.

This is something I can't fix for them. So, I stay in my bedroom while Silas pads barefoot and half-naked to confront my son downstairs and I resist the temptation to hover in the stairwell in the hopes of eavesdropping on their conversation.

Instead, I go to my bathroom and clean up. I dispose of the condom. I swipe a wet washcloth over my cock. My erection has long gone down, obviously, and I try very hard not to think about how close I was to unloading in Silas's tight, sweet ass before my inconsiderate, self-centered son appeared in my bedroom doorway.

I look at my reflection in the mirror. Jesus Christ. My son just caught me balls-deep in his ex-boyfriend, a boy young enough to be another of my sons. And I didn't stop fucking him when I saw him. I didn't try to cover up or hide what we were doing. I didn't even immediately tell him to get out of my private space.

No, instead, I put Silas on display in front of his ex-boyfriend and I made my son watch while I made his ex come. I whispered five words into Silas's ear that I knew would make him come and I kept him impaled on my cock while he did so.

I *wanted* Lance to see us. I wanted him to see what this beautiful boy looks like when he comes for a man who truly appreciates him. Who loves everything about him.

And that's the thought that makes me stare at myself in the mirror. I love Lance, despite my disappointment in his recent behavior, the way a father loves a son. And I thought I'd come to love Silas as Lance's boyfriend, as a father-in-law would love his son's partner.

But I love Silas the way a lover would. The way a Daddy loves his boy. And it's not about our age difference. I can see Silas growing older, gaining confidence, growing into the lean, coltish body he has. Getting laugh lines around those pretty eyes and that pouting, fuckable mouth. Going silver at his temples or losing his hair or putting on a few pounds around his middle. Even when all these things happen, he'll still be my boy. Even when he finds his place in the world, in the career he chooses, and makes a name for himself the way I know he will, I'll still be his Daddy.

I have every respect for the man he is now and the man he'll become. I don't think of him as less than my equal because he's twenty-five years my junior. I want to take care of him at home —and in bed—so he can go out and take care of everything else in his life.

But I don't know if he wants that. He shouldn't, probably. He shouldn't tie himself to a man so much older than him. He should be out there, clubbing or whatever it is kids his age do these days. Meeting new people, testing out what he wants with men his own age. Even if the thought of Silas looking up at another man and calling him *Daddy* makes me so jealous I can't see straight.

I don't know how to tell him how I feel about him. I *can't* tell him how I feel about him. Not yet, anyway. Not until he's had some time to get over Lance.

I leave the bathroom and pull my lounge pants and T-shirt back on. I change the sheets and make the bed. I'm still waiting for the boys to finish their conversation.

There's a burst of laughter from Lance's room and I am dying to know what the hell is going on between them. I suppose laughter is better than shouting? I hope so.

Finally, I hear footsteps in the downstairs hall and the front door opening and closing. Lance doesn't come to talk to me and I don't call out to him. I hardly know what to say to him and I think we can both wait a bit before we talk. My current priority is Silas.

I give him exactly five minutes to come to me, watching the second hand ticking around the face of my watch, and when he doesn't, I go to him.

He's lying facedown on Lance's bed and I can't tell whether he's crying or not. Hell, he could be sleeping—an adrenaline crash after the sex we've been having and an emotional confrontation would not be out of the realm of possibility.

I rap my knuckles on the doorframe. "Silas?"

He turns over immediately and sits up. His eyes are dry, but his hair is sticking up on one side of his head and a few strands are clinging to his other cheek.

"He's gone."

"I figured. Are you all right, sweetheart?"

Silas casts his eyes around Lance's room as if looking at it for the last time, trying to fix it in his memory. "I don't know," he says slowly. "I got the revenge I wanted. Don't think Lance really cared that much, though. He hasn't wanted me for a while now." He says it with a bitter twist to his mouth, then sighs. "Guess I'll move my shit out of his place next week."

"Where?" I start to ask, and Silas huffs a silent laugh, his narrow shoulders hunching forward.

"He says he came up to ask you if I could stay for a while." He gestures at the bed he's sitting on, the dresser that's been in Lance's room since he was in high school, and the shelf of sports trophies of the same vintage. "Here, I guess. I don't think he meant in your room." He giggles softly. "He was really surprised to find us fucking. Not even Lance could fake that expression."

"Lance was going to ask me to let you stay here?" I'm surprised, but this is actually consistent with the son I thought I'd raised. It's a little fucked up, considering what's happened between Silas and me, but at least Lance still cares enough about Silas to make sure he is taken care of. Even if it is his fault Silas needs a new place to stay.

Silas nods. "He said that no matter what happened between us, his dad would take care of me."

I take a few steps into the room, closer to the bed. "You know that's true, sweetheart. You knew it when you came here. I'll always take care of you, if you need me."

Silas brushes his hair back from his face and looks up at me. "Yeah. He didn't really like thinking about you taking care of me with your dick, though."

"No, I expect not," I say dryly.

I take another few steps closer. Close enough that I can reach out and run my hand through Silas's hair. He leans his head into my hand and gives a giant sigh, the kind that comes after a big emotional upheaval.

"Come on, baby," I say. "Let's have some dinner. You need to eat something."

Twenty-Two

SILAS

"YEAH," I SIGH. "Okay."

I don't feel hungry, but after everything that's happened, I probably do need to eat or something. I feel a little light-headed, maybe. A little disconnected, sort of, from whatever it is that tethers me to the earth.

I look up at Logan, who's standing patiently above me, holding out his hand to pull me up off the bed.

I put my hand in his. "Daddy?"

It's not like Logan hasn't been focused on me pretty much this entire weekend, and yet, the way his attention snaps to me when I say that is…well, I don't know what the hell it is, but it makes my chest tighten like I'm having trouble breathing.

"Would you…?" I cup my hand over my crotch fleetingly. I can't really bring myself to ask for it, but Logan's eyes soften and he brushes some hair back from my forehead.

"Of course, baby boy. Come on."

His big hand closes over mine and he tugs me to my feet. He leads me back upstairs to his bedroom, and sets me gently on the end of the bed.

"I'll be right back, sweetheart."

He goes off to—I don't even know, wherever he put it earlier —and comes back with the cage in his hand.

He kneels at the foot of the bed and drops the cage on the mattress near my right hip. "Let's get these off, baby, all right?"

He unbuttons my jeans, then works them down my legs when I stand. I put one hand on his shoulder for balance while he strips me out of them, then sit down on the edge of the bed again.

He pushes me gently with the flat of his hand on my chest, and I fall back like the first in a line of dominoes. My legs part and he runs a soothing hand up the inside of my thigh. He knows me well enough by now that if he touches me more than necessary, he's not going to be able to get me in it, so his fingers barely whisper over my balls before he scoops them into the cage. Then he tucks my barely stiffening dick in through the metal rings and brings the pieces together.

"There's my good boy." He tightens the bolt that closes the cage with the Allen wrench and strokes his fingers softly over my skin where it presses between the rings of the cage. My dick is soft and pink and looks so...protected in the cage. Like nothing can get to me to harm me.

Logan holds the Allen wrench out to me.

"You keep it, Daddy." I look up at him. "Please."

I can't handle any responsibility right now. I just want— need—someone—Logan—to take care of me.

Logan's fingers slowly close over the wrench and his knuckles go white with how hard he's clenching his fist. He doesn't say anything, though, just drops the wrench into a pocket in his lounge pants. He stands up and hugs me against his middle, hard, then kisses the top of my head.

"Just a second, baby," he murmurs against my hair and I nod.

He pulls away and I'm naked, caged, and bereft for a few cold seconds, but then he's back. He's got a pair of sweatpants and a T-shirt folded over an arm. The sweatpants are gray and look soft and cozy. He kneels in front of me again, strokes a hand down my leg to my ankle, and tucks my foot into one of the legs. He does the same with the other leg, then tugs me to my feet so he can pull the sweatpants up over my hips.

They're way looser than my jeans, which gives plenty of room for the cage, and they'd probably fall off me if it weren't for the elastic at the ankles and waist. There's a drawstring, too, and Logan pulls it snug, then ties it in a tidy bow.

He gathers the T-shirt's fabric between his large hands and stretches the neck opening wide enough to get over my head. I'm perfectly capable of dressing myself and I probably should, but I let my Daddy lift each arm into the shirt sleeves and pull it down over my stomach. He smoothes the blue fabric over my chest and kisses my forehead.

"Dinner," he says firmly. "Come on."

I follow him downstairs to the kitchen and perch on the same stool I've been using since the morning after I got here. I feel like I've spent the whole weekend either eating or having sex. Which I guess is what I came for, right? The sex part, anyway.

It's been a super hot interlude in the midst of the disaster my life has suddenly turned into, but it ends tomorrow and I still don't know what the hell I'm going to do.

"So, where have you been staying?" Logan's buttering the other half of the baguette left over from last night's dinner. I focus on his hands as he peels a clove of garlic, cuts it in half, and rubs the cut side along the buttered bread.

"With my friend Chloe," I say. "On an air mattress that takes up most of the floor in her tiny bedroom. Believe me, she hasn't been missing me this weekend."

"Oh, to be young enough to be able to sleep on an air mattress again," Logan murmurs almost to himself. He slides the garlic buttered bread under the broiler and scoops out two bowls of the meat and bean stew he made last night.

"How much stuff do you have to move?"

I sigh. "My clothes and shit. Laptop, monitor, all my computer stuff. My keyboard and French horn. This chair that I found in a secondhand store in Brooklyn that's super comfortable but Lance hates because he says it's ugly as fuck."

Lance picked most of the furniture. Or, the decorator who furnished the condo when his trust fund bought it did. She did a fine job—she didn't go overboard with anything and most of it came from Room and Board or Design Within Reach. It's this whole mid-century modern aesthetic and it looks nice and all. It's just not my style.

Not that I've had much opportunity to figure out my style. I went from home to the dorms to Lance's apartment. I've never actually lived on my own before. Shit, I'm going to have to find a roommate, aren't I? Maybe Chloe knows someone who's looking for one.

"The main thing is my books," I tell Logan. I read a lot and I also collect books about Broadway musicals. The hardcover, coffee-table kind of books that are filled with photos and annotated librettos and interviews with the original casts and things like that. "There's a wall of shelves in the living room of Lance's condo that's filled with mostly my books."

"I've seen it," Logan says. "That's a lot of books."

"And crap, all my sheet music." I've got a big, wooden, lateral file cabinet that's nearly filled with sheet music, method books, and scores. I started taking piano lessons in second grade and took up the French horn in middle school, so I've acquired a lot of music. Most of my own stuff I've composed is digital, at least.

Logan pulls the garlic bread from the oven and sets a heated-up bowl of stew in front of me. He pours himself a glass of wine but gives me a tall glass of water, which I drink without argument. I start eating when Logan settles in the stool next to me.

"Silas, will you let me help you?"

Logan sounds surprisingly hesitant, especially after taking charge of everything this weekend.

"You'd let me stay here?" I ask. "And store my shit? Like Lance suggested?"

"Well, I was thinking—" There's a sharp trill of a cell phone ringtone. It's not mine, since I turned the ringer off, so it must be Logan's. He gets off the stool and goes to the little alcove where he keeps the charger, turns the phone right side up, and then lifts it to his ear.

"Give me two minutes and I'll call you back."

Whoever it is says something affirmative that's cut off when Logan hangs up and then he looks at me with an expression I can't read.

"I have to take this, but when I'm done, we're going to have a talk."

"Um, okay." I'm definitely not in a position to demand all of Logan's attention this weekend. He said on Friday night that he was going to have one of his associates do the research he'd been planning to do this weekend. Probably that's them, reporting on their work. Of course I can entertain myself while he does the work I've been keeping him from.

"Finish your dinner." He points at my half-eaten bowl of meat and beans. He's already finished his.

"Yes, Daddy," I say.

He snags his half-drunk wine glass, then kisses my cheek when he passes me on the way to the stairs. "I won't be long, sweetheart. I promise."

Twenty-Three

LOGAN

I TAP THE name in the recent calls list on my phone as soon as I leave the kitchen. "Sorry about that," I say when the call connects.

"No prob," James says.

I reach my study and close the door. Hopefully, I'll have good news for Silas by the time he finishes his dinner. I doubt that James would be calling me on a Sunday if he wasn't interested.

"So?" I ask after I reach my desk and sit down at the chair behind it.

"I love it! It's fucking batshit, but it's brilliant. It's gonna be bigger than *The Lion King!*" James Cohen speaks mostly in hyperbole, but he knows the industry and his instincts are usually right.

"I thought you'd like it." He's been a client of mine for a decade or so and I've gotten to know him pretty well over that time.

"Where the hell did you find it? Who wrote it? Who's their rep?"

"His name is Silas Mitchell. He graduated from NYU Tisch last spring. And I guess I'm his rep. At least for now."

Fortunately or unfortunately, James knows me well, too, and his tone sharpens. "Wait, why are you representing some unknown composer and lyricist? You're normally production counsel, aren't you?"

I do normally represent Broadway producers or more established authors in the industry. Most often, I'm on the other side of the table from the young up-and-coming bookwriters, lyricists, or composers trying to break into the business. Not that I'm ever out to screw them, but my clients' interest is typically in maximizing the return on their investment and minimizing to the extent possible within industry standards the advances or royalties paid to the talent and creative teams.

"He's been working on this for a year or so," I tell James. "It's not quite there yet, but I knew you'd see the potential. Still, if you're not interested, I can connect him with Jeffrey Seller."

James and Seller have gotten into bidding wars before on new material, so I know that's like waving a red cloak before a bull.

"Don't you dare—I said I was interested! Just—Logan, who the hell is this kid? What's your angle here?"

"I think the boy has talent, that's all. He deserves a chance." Jesus, that sounds lame even to my own ears.

"The kind of chance a recent theater grad would give his left nut for," James says, and he's not wrong. Still, this business is eighty percent who you know, as James himself very well knows. "Whose dick did he suck to get your attention?"

I don't answer immediately and James takes my silence for a confession. "Oh, Logan. You didn't! You dirty dog, you!"

"I'm not," I protest, but I'm actually a terrible liar. I can keep a poker face when representing my clients and I have no trouble keeping their confidences, but I can't actually lie, especially to my friends. And James is probably the closest friend I have.

"I— He— We—" Fuck. So much for my professional eloquence.

"When did you meet him? Last I heard, it was all one-night stands and Grindr hookups for you. You haven't seen anyone more than a couple of times in how long?"

"I've known him for two years," I say truthfully. "But we've only just gotten together." Also true, even if us being together is supposed to be just for the weekend. But whatever happens between us, Silas deserves this chance to advance his career in ways that I can help.

"Wait, if you've known him for two years and he just graduated from Tisch...Jesus, Logan, how old is he?"

"Twenty-two," I say. I let the phone fall away from my ear and take a sip of wine while James cackles loud enough that I glance at my study door to make sure it's still closed.

I don't tell James that it's worse than me trading on my connections for a boy I'm fucking who's young enough to be my son. That he was my son's boyfriend first and that his ass is probably still sore from the pounding I gave it earlier today and that if I have my way, I'll keep pounding that ass as long as he lets me.

"Wait a minute," James says. "You said his name is Silas? Wasn't that the kid at your firm's holiday party? The one who drank the caterers out of Jameson?"

Shit. I forgot that I'd pulled Silas away from talking to James when I went to collect him and take him home. "Yes," I admitted. "That's him." Christ, I hope I'd managed to reach him before he spilled the whole sordid story to James.

There's a beat of silence, but James doesn't reveal anything else about that night, just tsks at me on the other end of the call. "I hope you know what you're doing here, friend."

I'm doing this because I'm in love with him and to equalize our relationship as much as I can so that he has the resources to live his life without me if he wants.

"Well?" I ask James. "Are you in?"

"Fucking yes, I'm in. Don't tell me I gotta find a new lawyer, though?"

"Call Adrienne." She's one of the other partners at my firm and James is right—I can't represent him in this deal if I'm looking out for Silas's interests. "I'll give her a heads up to expect you."

I need to get Silas his own representation, too. It's not kosher, ethically speaking, to represent him while I'm fucking him.

We spitball a few more details—names of potential directors and general managers, a choreographer that James likes to work with but who might be busy with another show—then wind the call up. I send a quick email to Adrienne, giving her the bare bones of the deal and leaving out the details of my relationship with Silas, just that I'm conflicted out of representing James. She'll find out why eventually, but for now, she can get started drafting the standard production contract.

I drain the last few swallows of my wine and think about how to present this deal and my other proposals to Silas. I could wait until I have a draft production contract in hand to show him. The basic terms are standard in the industry, and, as a member of the Dramatists Guild, Silas might already be familiar with most of them. I'll try to get him higher advance payments than the minimum terms, though I expect James will push hard on that, since this is Silas's first musical.

I open my laptop and log onto the firm's network and scroll through archived files of previous deals. I click around a few files, looking at riders that supplement deals I think are similar to this one. I'm killing time, I know—putting off the moment when I tell Silas everything I've put in motion. He's been amenable to me dominating him for the weekend, but this is his career and life I'm talking about.

Will he let me take charge of everything? There's only one way to find out.

I scoop my laptop under one arm and snag my empty wine glass in my other hand and return to the kitchen. Except Silas isn't there.

Our dishes are cleared away from the island countertop and the dishwasher is quietly humming its cycle.

Silas isn't in the living room, but he's been in the music room, because he's cleaned that up, too. The blank manuscript paper has been tidied away and there's just the pages he used to write down the song he was working on stacked neatly on the piano's music rack. If he agrees to my plan, I'll need to make some space for him.

I have a hunch where he might be, so I head back to the main level. To Lance's bedroom. The door is half-closed and I don't hear anything coming from inside, but when I peek around the door, Silas is sitting on the end of Lance's bed. His phone is in his hands and he's tapping away with his thumbs at lightning speed.

His hair is hanging in his face, like it seems to do all the time, and he has a look of deep concentration on his face. And then the corners of his mouth lift and he snorts quietly at something he's reading on his phone. Texting his friend, I presume.

It's too much like eavesdropping to stay here and watch him, so I leave him to his phone and whoever he's texting with and head back to the living room. I can wait until he's ready to come to me.

Twenty~Four

SILAS

I MIGHT AS well check in with Chloe while Logan is on his call. I take my phone into Lance's bedroom and perch on the end of his bed. Despite everything, this is the room I've spent the most time in and I need a place to think.

> Hey

I text her. It's only a few seconds before she texts back.

> hey cupcake!

> tired of boning mr. reynolds already?

I'm never going to tire of that, but I'm the one who told her this was just for the weekend and nothing serious. Except that it's getting serious, at least for me, and I really don't know what to do about it.

She also uses emojis way more than necessary. As I'm looking down at my phone, a series of cartoon images pop up one after the other and it takes me a minute to figure some of them out.

> Why are you sending me eggplants?

> And...water droplets?

Then something I have to squint at for a minute before realizing it's meant to be fireworks, a burning cigarette, a cartoon face with a hand over a yawning mouth, and then another face with a bunch of zzzs floating over its head.

> Ha.

I text back.

> Very subtle.

when are you coming home?

> Uh, I'm not sure.

I really need to talk some of this shit out, but I hit decline when Chloe calls.

> Texts, pls.

um, okay.

Three dots dance on the screen while Chloe types.

wait, are you safe?

why can't you talk?

> I'm fine. Logan's upstairs on a work call.

okay.

and?

> And I dunno when he'll get off and I don't want him to overhear.

> overhear what?

> I'm sort of having an existential crisis.

She sends a heart emoji.

> why are you having an existential crisis, cupcake?

I start typing but really, I have no idea how to explain this. Or even what it is. When several seconds go by and I haven't sent anything, Chloe starts typing herself.

> you said this was just for the weekend and no big deal. i gather that's changed?

She's like the most perceptive person I know.

> Yeah.

> But it's complicated.

Explaining to Chloe that I'm letting Lance's dad be my Daddy, at least for the weekend, is the very definition of complicated.

> oh my god, are you letting lance's dad be your daddy?

Well, crap. I guess not that complicated.

> Um...

I mean, she knows me pretty well and I don't keep a lot of secrets from her but damn, I didn't expect her to guess this immediately.

> holy shit!

Another set of three dots bounce but only for a second before there's another flurry of emojis. A cartoon version of a dad with a little boy in front of him, another eggplant, and then a cartoon face of a baby, complete with a single curl on the top of its head.

And then a baby bottle, an open safety pin, and the emoji face with the raised eyebrow.

> OMG, was that meant to be a diaper pin? WTF, it's not like that!

> dude, don't yuck someone else's yum.

> Dude, baby bottles and diapers are not my yum!

> whatevs.

> why complicated?

> Well, for one thing, Lance walked in on us.

Okay, I'm a coward, but I'm easing into it. Or something.
Chloe sends a whole slew of laughing/crying emojis.

> That's not very nice.

> that dicknose nut hound isn't very nice.

A giggle escapes my lips and I glance at the door, hoping Logan is still on the phone upstairs. It takes me a few seconds to get back to our text convo.

> you still haven't explained what's complicated.

I know. Oh, the hell with it. Logan's going to get off his call eventually and I did start texting her to talk about this.

He says he wants to help me.

who, lance?

would have helped immensely if he hadn't cheated on you.

No, Logan.

I mean, Lance was trying to help me in his way, but that's obviously not what I'm talking about.

help you with what?

Not 100% sure.

We were having dinner and he said "will you let me help you?"

But then his phone rang and he said he had to take the call and...

and you're not sure if he meant help you with his dick or something else.

like his money, maybe?

Something like that, yeah.

what do you want from him, hon?

I sigh and toss my phone on Lance's bed, then flop onto my back. I have no idea what I want from Logan.

Yeah, that's a lie. I want everything. But what if Logan only wants to help me out of some sort of guilt because it's his son who cheated on me and left me needing to find a new apartment and a better-paying job?

My phone buzzes next to me and I lift it over my face to read Chloe's new text.

??????

I dunno, dude.

why is it a problem that your sugar daddy boyfriend wants to help you?

isn't that what daddies do?

Because—boyfriend?? Is that what he is? I mean, two days ago he was my boyfriend's dad.

and you've had a crush on him since you met him.

plus, you've been wanting to find a nice daddy.

and you deserve a better boyfriend than that pompous prick goblin.

I'm in said pompous prick goblin's childhood bedroom, texting my best friend and agonizing over what I want from his dad. Why is it so hard to admit what I want?

silas, do you want him to be your boyfriend daddy or not?

I take a deep breath and jab at each letter, then hit send before I lose my nerve.

Yes.

there, was that so hard?

Oh my god, so hard. But freeing in a way. Like, now that I've admitted to myself what I want, I can finally start to imagine it.

has he said anything about how he feels about you?

other than that he wants to help you?

Um, not exactly. But he said he'll always take care of me if I need him.

that sounds good!

doesn't it?

Yeah.

I think about everything Logan's said or done this weekend and none of it feels temporary. He hasn't pushed me for more than I've been willing to give. He's just...been here the whole time.

Taking care of me. Feeding me, making sure I drink water and not too much alcohol. Letting me catch up on my sleep, letting me work on my musical when I wanted to. I showed up on his doorstep on Friday night with no warning and he rearranged his entire weekend to be everything I didn't know I needed.

My hands brush against the hard metal of the cock cage under my—Logan's—sweatpants. I honestly think he bought it just for kinky fun, but it didn't take either of us long to realize how it affects my head as much as my body.

He knew that it would help settle me after my confrontation with Lance. I barely had to ask for it and he just...took care of what I needed, the way he's done this whole weekend.

I tap my phone screen, which has gone dark while I've been sitting here and tap out one more text to Chloe.

I gotta go talk to him.

She sends me the thumbs-up emoji, then the fingers-crossed one, and then a huge smiley face.

call me later, cupcake.

I will but I don't bother responding. I shove my phone in my pocket and leave Lance's bedroom to go find Logan.

He's in the dining room, at the end with the puzzle. I wonder what his phone call was about that he needs to think things over afterwards while working on the puzzle.

He looks up when I enter the room and I drift across the rug to lean against his chair. He's finished the lighthouse and added more sky pieces. My eye catches on a weird-shaped piece with a touch of blue that's sitting atop the pile in the box and I snap it into place to complete the blueberries.

It's one of the things I like about jigsaw puzzles—that you can look and look for the right pieces, but sometimes, if you walk away for a bit, when you come back, the piece you've been looking for is right there.

"Nice," Logan says. He sets down the piece he's holding and pushes his chair back. "We need to talk, sweetheart."

"Yeah," I agree, but first, he beckons me closer.

"Let's get the cage off. You've been in it for a while and I need your full attention, because there are some decisions you need to make."

Well, that doesn't sound ominous or anything. Still, I shuffle toward him and he tugs my sweatpants down enough to expose my caged cock. His hands are warm as he reaches under me with the Allen wrench to loosen it. He gently extracts my dick and balls, and naturally, I—ahem—rise to the occasion in his hand.

"Sorry," I murmur, but he just chuckles and sets the cage on the table.

"Later," he promises my dick. Then he kisses my stomach and pulls the sweatpants up, stretching the waistband wide enough to deny me even the soft friction the fabric might otherwise give and re-ties the drawstring. "We've got some things to discuss first."

"Okay, but can I start?" If I don't get this out asap, I'll lose my nerve. Also, I don't know what Logan is planning to say, but I kind of want to make my case first, in case he's planning to send me off for my own good.

He glances at his laptop, which is on the coffee table in front of the sofa—the sofa that we've done a lot of dirty things on this weekend—but nods. "Of course, Silas."

I take a deep breath. Shit, I haven't really thought about what to say or how to say it. "Um, so this weekend has been awesome and everything."

Logan laces his fingers together and rests them in his lap. He looks up at me, standing in front of him, wearing his clothes that he dressed me in, and I want to crawl into his lap and let him say the hard things, but he's been doing that for me the whole weekend and it's my turn to man up here.

"I didn't plan on anything more than a night with you when I came here." I drag my hand through my hair, pushing it off my face. "Shit, I didn't actually think you'd do anything with me. I kind of figured you'd pat me on the head, let me bitch a little about Lance, and send me home with some fatherly advice like *it'll get better* and *you'll find someone new soon* or whatever."

Logan's mouth twists into a half smile. "That's probably what I should have done," he says quietly, almost to himself. He drops his eyes to his hands in his lap and I see that his fingers are clenched around each other and his knuckles are turning white.

"But instead, you gave me the hottest, sexiest," I let my voice drop to a whisper, "dirtiest weekend of kinky sex that I've ever had. And you didn't even get to come when you finally fucked me."

His eyes snap up to mine. "Oh, Silas, please tell me you haven't been worrying about that. Orgasms are nice and all, but I promise you, that is not a problem."

"What I'm saying," I interrupt him. "Is that you've been taking care of me and prioritizing what *I* want the whole weekend and you deserve to have your needs met, too."

"And that's wonderful of you, sweetheart, but—"

"Are you going to let me finish?" I cross my arms over my chest.

Logan opens his mouth and then shuts it. He mimes zipping his lips closed with two fingers and re-laces his hands together in his lap.

"All right, then." Now I do crawl into his lap, straddling his thighs and draping my arms over his shoulders. His hands hover on either side of me for a second before he carefully settles them on my hips. My dick, which had softened while I was talking, perks up at the nearness of Logan's. I ignore it for now.

"I think I love you." I say it quickly on an out breath. "I want you to be my Daddy for more than just this weekend. And also, you know…maybe, like, my boyfriend. I know it'll be weird with Lance and everything, and maybe you don't want to tell anyone about us, especially at work and everything, and I totally get that, but—"

Logan cuts me off when he tightens his arms and pulls me to him. He squeezes me against his chest tight enough that I can't breathe, not to mention that my nose is smushed into his collarbone.

"Baby boy," he whispers against the side of my head. "I love you too. More than you have any idea."

I relax against him and his arms loosen enough that I can turn my head and breathe a little easier. I close my eyes and take in the scent of his skin behind his ear, the product he uses for his hair and beard, his laundry detergent.

He smells like home.

I DON'T KNOW how long I hold Silas. Long enough that my legs start to tingle from his weight in my lap, but I don't care. He fits perfectly here and he's agreed to be mine.

Silas's weight settles even more and he sighs. I shift my legs a bit and jostle him. "You're not falling asleep, are you?"

"No," he murmurs sleepily.

"Don't lie to me, boy," I say, but I don't put any command behind it and I can feel his lips curve into a smile against my neck.

I loosen my arms and tap his hip. "Come on, baby. There are still some things we need to talk about."

He straightens up, shaking his head to wake himself up, his hair flopping around his face. "Oh. Right. What did you want to talk about?"

I give him a gentle push and he slides off my lap without complaint. "Let's sit on the sofa."

When we're settled there next to each other, I pull my laptop closer and open the lid. I call up the two tabs in my browser I want him to see and swivel the laptop to him. I start with the bank website, logged into the account dashboard. "This is yours. The debit card will come in the mail in a couple days.

It's linked to my account for deposits, but you have full control of it to do with as you please."

Silas's mouth opens and he starts to say something, but I put my hand on his knee. "Give me a second, please? Trust me."

He closes his mouth and nods, though he looks on the verge of protesting. I switch to the apartment listings. "I assumed you want to stay in Manhattan, but if you'd rather live in Brooklyn or one of the other boroughs, we can change the search locations."

"Brooklyn?" Silas echoes. "No, I mean...Wait, what?" He leans forward and reads a few descriptions of the amenities in the apartments on the list. "On-site gym...roof deck with incredible views...bike room..." He looks sideways at me. "Logan, I can't afford these apartments."

"Sweetheart, I can. The list is already filtered to the maximum I'm willing to pay. This is not a hardship for me, Silas. I want to take care of you."

I turn toward him, bending a knee and pulling it up on the sofa. "We can stay here or in my Upper West Side condo whenever you want, but I want you to have a place that's yours. Just like I want you to have money that is yours alone to control. You might be my boy, but this isn't an allowance. This is my way of sharing my life with you."

Silas looks between the laptop screen with its list of apartments and me several times before saying anything. "I...Logan, I don't want you to think I'm only interested in you for your money."

I laugh. I shouldn't, because Silas hunches in on himself, but I can't help it. "Oh baby, I know that." I'm going to hold him again in a minute, but first I lean forward, swivel the laptop toward me, and click open my email.

There's a new message at the top of my inbox from Adrienne. Excellent. I open the attachment and turn the laptop back so Silas can read it.

His eyes flit back and forth, reading the first part of the contract. His lips move, silently spelling out "Approved Production Contract," a term he must know as a member of the Dramatists Guild, then his eyes jump back to the top of the document, which lists the parties to the contract.

"James Cohen?"

"Yes," I say.

"The Broadway producer?"

"Yes."

"The one who's produced, like half of the last dozen big hits on Broadway?"

"Yes."

"Doesn't he have, like, ten Tony awards?"

I shrug. "I don't know how many he has. Should I call him back and ask?"

"Call him back?" Silas's head jerks around to face me. "Wait, you asked James freaking Cohen to produce my musical?"

"No. I sent your musical to James and he called me and said he wants to produce it."

Silas stares at me like he doesn't know what to say. "James has been a client for a decade or more," I tell him. "I know what he likes."

Silas still doesn't say anything, though his brows are drawing together and he's starting to frown a little. I shift closer to him.

"Sweetheart, James is an experienced producer. You said it yourself, he's produced half of the last dozen Broadway hits." And more than a few shows that closed within the opening week, but I don't mention that. "He has his pick of shows and he knows what he wants. If he wasn't truly interested in your musical, he would have told me so."

"But he only looked at it because you sent it to him."

"True. But do you think I'm the first or only person who's sent him something to read?"

He sighs. "It's not what you know, it's who you know. Right."

"Baby, I didn't tell him about us when I sent it to him. Yes, he looked at it because I sent it to him, but he made his own decision about it before he knew anything about us. And he wants to produce it because he thinks it's brilliant. That's the word he used when he called me."

Silas still looks like he's been hit between the eyes. "What?"

I put my hands on either side of his face and lift it to look at me. "James Cohen thinks your musical is brilliant and wants to produce it on Broadway, Silas."

"James Cohen?" he repeats. His voice is weak, but his eyes light up. "James freaking Cohen thinks my musical is brilliant?"

"Yes."

"And he wants to put it on Broadway?" His voice tips higher at the end in his excitement.

"Yes."

"Holy fucking shit!" He jumps up from the sofa and dances around the living room. I'm grinning ear to ear watching him. He spins and punches the air a few times, then does this little dance that's almost an old-fashioned soft-shoe bit, all the while chanting, "James freaking Cohen! James. Freaking. Cohen!"

He stops after a few minutes and bends over to catch his breath, his hands on his knees. Then he straightens up, tosses his hair out of his face, and settles back on the sofa next to me. He's wiped the look of glee off and is attempting to look serious, but there's still a manic glint in his eyes.

"Sorry, it's like, Christmas, my birthday, and Fourth of July all rolled into one."

"It's a big deal, sweetheart. You have every right to be excited."

He leans forward to look at the laptop screen again. "So, where do I sign?"

I stroke the long line of his back. "You need to read it first, Silas. Yes, it's the standard contract, but there are still things you can negotiate. I'll set up a meeting for you with Susannah Sondberg and she'll help you figure out a reasonable counteroffer."

Silas scrolls through the pages of the contract but I can tell he's too excited to take in all the words. "When?" he asks, still scrolling.

"Later this week, probably. Depends on Susannah's schedule, of course."

"No, I mean when would it start? The performances?" He swivels his head to look at me, one finger still resting on the laptop's keypad. "It's not ready, Logan. I mean, I just rewrote that song for Act Two, and I don't think the transition to Act Three is working at all right now, and there's no choreography or anything—I don't even know anything about choreography —and—"

He runs out of breath and I rub soothing strokes up and down his back. "Relax, baby. It'll be months before the show is ready to go onstage. There's plenty of time to make changes until you and James are completely satisfied. James will hire a choreographer and you'll have a say in everything."

Silas sits back against the sofa cushions and stares at the laptop. Then he looks at me. "This is really going to happen? For real?"

I take his hand and thread my fingers between his. "There are still a number of things to work out. And James has to raise the money to produce the show first. But this," I tip my head at the laptop with the contract displayed on the screen, "is the beginning of making it happen. For real."

"Wow." Silas squeezes my hand. I let him sit there for a few minutes and bask in the news that someday a musical that he wrote will be performed on Broadway. All I did was open the door to this dream, but I can't help but bask myself in the small role that I'm able to play.

Finally, I lift his hand and kiss his knuckles. "So, you see, baby, that I'm not worried that you're only interested in me for my money." Silas glances at me. He's possibly forgotten what he said earlier. "If anything, you should be worried that I'm only interested in you because you're going to be famous." I wink at him and he scoffs.

"No one ever remembers who wrote a musical, just who stars in it." And then he sits up straight. "Oh my god, who is going to star in it? Do I get a say in that?"

I chuckle and point to the contract on the screen. "Guess you'll have to read that and find out."

Silas bounces in his seat a few times, then settles. He blows a breath out, stirring the hair that continually flops over his face, and turns to me. "Thank you," he says. He looks at the laptop and then back at me. "For…all of this. It's too much, really, and I have no idea how to repay you."

I cup his cheek in my hand. "Silas, there's no repayment. The apartment is so that I know my boy is safe. The money is temporary, until you're earning what you need on your own, and I can afford both. And speaking of money, you should take a look at the advance figures in that contract. Susannah might even be able to negotiate a little more. And the connection to James is because I know how talented you are. I merely know other people who also see that."

He rubs his cheek against my palm, then turns his head and kisses the center of it. He drops his eyes to my crotch, looks back up at me through the fall of his bangs, and grins wickedly. "Well, there is one way I can thank you, Daddy."

My cock hardens immediately. He sees it and his tongue peeks out from between his lips. "You don't need to thank me, Silas," I manage. "Not like this, I mean."

He blinks his eyes at me and, with those long lashes and that pouting mouth, I'm sunk. I know it. He knows it.

"Oh, come on," he says. "Let's play casting couch." He draws his knees up onto the sofa and swivels toward me, sitting sideways.

"Casting couch?" I turn sideways, too, and face him.

"You know what I mean." He bats his eyelashes again, like a cartoon pin up model. "Oh, Mr. Reynolds, I'd do just about *anything* for the chance to see my musical on Broadway." He puts on a terrible Southern belle accent. It's barely recognizable as such.

What the hell. I'll play along. "Anything?" I stroke my chin like a cartoon villain mulling over his crimes. Silas stifles a smirk. "Well, that's a pretty big deal, you know—getting a musical produced on Broadway," I say. "Seems like you'd need to be pretty talented if I were to make that happen for you."

Silas shoves the coffee table back with one foot and drops to his knees on the floor before the sofa. He shimmies around until he's between my knees and pushes my legs wider to make room for himself.

"Oh, I think you'll find that I'm very—" he licks his lips —"*very* talented, Mr. Reynolds. Sir."

He gets my cock out in the blink of an eye and his mouth engulfs me in its wet heat. Then he shows me exactly how talented he is.

Twenty-Six

SILAS

THE THING I like best about sucking Logan's dick—especially when he's in charge of it—is how my brain just quits working while he's fucking my face. I don't have to think about anything while he's battering my throat and holding me still. All my worries drift away and there's nothing but the musky scent and tangy taste of him that blocks out everything else.

Except for one thought. When Logan lets me up to breathe, I manage to wheeze out, "Red."

Logan goes absolutely still and his hands immediately drop to his sides on the sofa. There's a pearl of fluid beading up at his slit, but he hauls in a deep breath, blows it out, and says, "Okay. Good boy."

I think he means that it's good that I remembered the stoplight system he suggested we use. Because I hope that he doesn't think it's good that I stopped blowing him right before he got to come. But I stopped for a reason and I just need to catch my breath to explain it to him.

I brace my hand on his thigh while I drag in a couple of deep breaths. My jaw aches in the best way and my throat is sore like I hope it will be a whole lot in the future. I get to have this whenever I want. Me on my knees before my Daddy. Him fucking my face and my ass whenever he decides to.

And that's exactly why I called *red.*

"I don't mean I want to stop," I say. My voice is wrecked—another thing I hope happens a lot in the future. "I just..." I cough a few times and swallow down the lump in my throat. "I want you to come inside me. I know you said it didn't matter that you didn't get to earlier, but I want to feel you like that."

Daddy cups my face in his hand and his thumb rubs just under my eye. "I didn't say it didn't matter," he murmurs. "Just that it wasn't a problem. Considering the circumstances, I'd be a pretty shitty Daddy if I blamed you for not being able to come inside you the last time."

"Then let's have a do over. We can pretend it's the first time and hopefully, we won't be interrupted again."

He snorts. "I suspect Lance won't be showing up here without warning again."

I'm still having trouble thinking about Lance without getting annoyed at him, but the pain is way less. He can have his meaningless blow jobs. I have my Daddy.

Who's lifting me to my feet and steering me to the stairs and I let the butterflies in my stomach at the prospect of Logan fucking me again flap away the last bit of anger at Lance.

When we get to his room, Daddy strips my clothes off and points to the bed. "On your back, boy, arms overhead."

I climb onto the bed, giving my ass a little shimmy as I do so, in the hopes that Daddy will spank me. He does, because he's the best Daddy in the world, but only once on each cheek. I lay down in the middle of the big bed and Logan goes to the nightstand.

He takes the lube from the drawer and sets it on the surface with a solid thump. He fishes a condom out, then looks at me with the foil package tucked between his fingers. "Are you okay with me bare?"

More than anything. "Yes, please, Daddy."

He tosses the condom back into the drawer and picks up the thin ropes he'd brought in the last time we were here. "I know you'll be a very good boy, but I want to tie you up. How do you feel about that?"

"Green, Daddy. Like Elphaba from *Wicked* green."

He grabs my wrists and matches them together in front of my chest, then wraps a doubled length of rope around my wrists. "Put your elbows together," he orders me.

I comply and the way my arms drag over my nipple rings, plus the anticipation of getting tied up, makes my dick jump. He wraps the rope around my wrists twice, then crosses the ends, and drapes the folded end between my hands and over the wraps around my wrists. He makes a loop with the trailing ends and tucks the folded ends through the loop, between my hands again, under the top set of wraps, and through the loop a second time.

He tugs on the trailing ends of the rope and tightens down the knot he's just made. "Wiggle your fingers for me, baby."

I do and they move easily. The rope is stiff and firm around my wrists but not compressing the blood flow to my fingers or the nerves in my wrists. I feel secure and safe within the bonds my Daddy made.

He pulls my arms up and over my head and secures the trailing ends of the rope to the headboard. The bed has four tall posts and the headboard and footboard have railings with vertical poles. Perfect for tying someone up in a bunch of different ways. I wonder how many boys Logan's tied up here before me, but then I push that thought away. It doesn't matter. He's mine now and everything he's done this weekend shows that he wants only me.

And I want him so freaking bad.

He's not done tying me up, though, apparently. He wraps another doubled length of rope around each ankle and secures the knots similar to how he did my wrists. Then he kneels up on the bed, grabs my right leg and bends it at the knee until my foot is planted snug against my ass. I can't see what he's doing very well, but I can feel his warm hands on my thigh and ankle and the rope sliding across my skin. He spirals the rope from my ankle around my thigh three times and does something to tuck the wraps together on the inside of my leg.

Then he does the same with my left leg and sits back on his heels to assess his handiwork. There's that tiny smile he gets when he looks at me and I just...settle. I'm splayed open to him, my dick lying hard and heavy on my stomach, my hole on display, and I can't do anything to stop him from taking me any way he wants.

It's the best feeling in the world.

"Such a pretty boy for me," Daddy murmurs. He puts his hands on my knees, adjusts my legs a smidge, and I relax into the ropes that hold me tight. He slides his hands down the inside of my thighs, bumping over the rope wraps, until he reaches my groin. He brackets my dick and balls with his big hands, tucks his thumbs behind my sac, and bends to blow a warm breath on the underside of my aching shaft.

Then he slides down the bed until his head is between my spread legs, lifts my balls out of the way, and licks a hot, wet stripe over my hole.

"Oh, yes, Daddy," I moan.

He takes his sweet time about it, licking me open, pressing at my taint with his thumbs, and I let the sensations wash over me. My nipples stiffen, my dick aches, and my balls draw up, but the rest of me is a gooey puddle of simmering pleasure.

I lose track of time while he licks and nibbles and prods at me with his tongue, until he comes up for air and stretches over me for the lube on the nightstand. He slicks his cock up, shuffles forward on his knees, and lines himself up at my entrance.

I'm so relaxed that the blunt head of his dick only burns a little as he presses forward. He pulls out, dribbles more lube over himself, then slides his hands under my hips and lifts me to meet him. He pushes inside me steadily, forcing my insides to rearrange to accommodate him until he's seated all the way.

My hole is stretched wide around my Daddy's cock and there's nothing I can do but lie here and take him. My skin flushes cold, then hot, and I'm waiting for him to move, but he's looking down and all I can see is the top of his head. His hair is mussed and there's a bit sticking up. I'd smooth it down if I had use of my hands, but I don't, so instead, I just look at how the silver strands mix with the dark ones and bask in the knowledge that I'm his.

"I wish you could see how pretty you look, stretched around my cock, baby boy." Logan finally looks at me and that tiny smile is back again. I smile back at him. My brain is too quiet to make words, but he seems to understand, because a look of satisfaction washes over his face. Like he knows why I can't speak, because he's the one who put me in this place where my brain doesn't have to work.

"I'm going to fuck you hard, baby. You tell me yellow or red if it's too much for you."

It won't be. I know it. I close my eyes in anticipation, but Logan says, "No. Eyes on me, boy. You can come whenever you want, but keep your eyes open and on me."

I almost come right then. I snap my eyes open and gaze at him. His expression is serious now, his eyebrows drawn together, his lips firm. He looks powerful and intimidating, despite being naked and the sheen of sweat glistening on his forehead.

He pulls out slowly, nearly all the way, until the fat head of his dick stretches me even more. Then he bends forward, plants one hand on the bed next to my armpit, slides the other farther under me to the small of my back, and shoves back inside me in one hard thrust.

He sets a punishing rhythm, driving from where his knees are wedged under my bound legs. His eyes bore into mine while he saws in and out, grinding over my prostate with almost every stroke. It burns and burns and there's no escape from it, or him, until it stops burning at my hole, but then it's fire licking along all my nerve endings.

My dick steadily leaks onto my belly. Sweat from Logan's chest drips onto me and mingles with my own sweat. I come eventually, my orgasm rolling over me like a tidal wave, and though my vision fades and the image of him above me swims in duplicate, I keep my eyes open, like he commanded me.

Logan ignores my softening dick and the come splashed all over both of us. He punches into me, over and over, harsh panting breaths washing over my heated skin, guttural moans and grunts in the back of his throat. I'm loose and pliant beneath him and his thrusts shake the bed and me in my bonds.

And then he shoves into me, hard, and stops. A long, low groan falls from his mouth and I feel him pulse inside me. He's still staring down at me and I'm as caught by the expressions of love and need and satisfaction on his face as I am in his ropes. If my legs were free, I'd wrap them around his hips to keep him here as long as I can.

Twenty-Seven

LOGAN

THE BUZZ OF my phone on the nightstand early Monday morning doesn't wake me, since I've been awake for a while now, playing with strands of Silas's hair and trying to decide how much work I can pass off on someone else so I can spend the day in bed with him.

It doesn't wake Silas, either, though he turns over within the circle of my arms and buries his head between the pillows.

I ease my arm from under him and turn over myself to snag the phone and check the display.

It's Lance.

Probably best if I take this now, while Silas is still asleep. I swing my legs from under the covers and disentangle the lounge pants I'd abandoned on the floor last night from the ropes that I'd tossed off the bed after untying Silas. I pull the pants on, grab the closest shirt to hand, then close the door softly behind me.

The call's gone to voicemail by the time I get downstairs but Lance's generation doesn't leave voice messages—it's a wonder he tried calling in the first place, instead of texting—so I tap the missed call notification and tuck the phone between my shoulder and ear to free my hands to start the coffee.

"Dad."

"Son."

There's silence on Lance's end and I let it stretch out while I fill the electric kettle and grind some beans for the French press.

"What's up?" I finally say.

A huff like Lance used to make when he was a surly teenager and then he says, "You're fucking my ex-boyfriend, Dad. That's what's up."

"Key word being 'ex' there, kiddo," I say. "And what the fuck, Lance? You couldn't have broken up with him before finding someone new to suck your cock?"

"I didn't..." Lance starts, then corrects himself before I have to argue with him. "I mean, okay, I did, but I didn't mean for it to go down like that. I didn't set out to cheat on him, Dad. Things haven't been working between me and Silas for a while, and I don't know, I just...got restless or something. It was a spur of the moment thing and it didn't even mean anything."

"It was a spur of the moment thing with a member of the catering staff my firm hired for its holiday party, Lance. Do you even understand the position you put me in?"

"I fucked up, Dad, I know. And I'm sorry. I already apologized to Silas. So, now I'm apologizing to you. And to your firm and whatever."

And whatever. At least it was only Silas and me who caught Lance with his dick down the cater-waiter's throat. I haven't heard any blowback from my other partners or from the executive assistant who worked with the catering company to plan the party. If the cater-waiter has any notion of self-preservation, he'll keep his mouth shut and his pants zipped to keep these kinds of jobs.

"All right, Lance. I appreciate the apology." I can't really say I've forgiven him yet. It's not my place to fight Silas's battles for him, and he's already had it out with Lance, but I sure as hell am not going to absolve Lance for what he did. Son or not, it was a shitty thing to do and I'm still disappointed in him. Lance doesn't push it.

The kettle boils and I pour the hot water over the grounds in the French press, then set the lid on top of the glass beaker. I tuck the phone between my ear and shoulder again and get a pan out, putting it on the burner. There's more silence between me and Lance, and I might as well start breakfast while we're not talking.

"So, um...Christmas," Lance finally starts. "I'm guessing you'll want to spend it with Silas." It's not exactly a question, because my son isn't an idiot. Even though he's done some stupid shit.

"We haven't talked about that yet, but..." It's the elephant in the room that we haven't yet broached, even after discussing other ways of sharing our lives together.

"Okay, well, I talked to Mom, and—"

"You what?"

"I called Mom," he repeats, a little impatiently. "And I told her that I kinda need to get away for a while and she said I could come visit. We'll spend Christmas in her flat in Paris and then maybe go to the Riviera for New Year's Eve."

Lance used to spend part of each summer with his mother in France, but as far as I knew, he hasn't seen her in a couple of years. "What did you tell her about why you need to get away?"

"I told her that I cheated on my boyfriend and we broke up. I didn't tell her anything about you and Silas." He makes a disgusted noise in the back of his throat. "Honestly, Dad, the less I have to think about you and Silas, the better. I don't think there's enough bleach in the world to scrub what I saw out of my head."

"And whose fault is that?"

"Jesus, Dad, how the hell was I to know you'd be balls-deep in my ex when I stopped by to talk to you on a Sunday afternoon?"

"Well, now you know how—"

"How Silas felt when he saw me." Lance interrupts, a trait I do not appreciate, but I let it slide this time. "I get it, Dad.

I do. And that's why I think it's best if I go somewhere else for Christmas. I know Silas's parents are going on some cruise or something and it's not fair for him to have to spend the holidays alone after what I did. But I really, really, *really* do *not* want to watch the two of you mooning over each other. Or worse."

He's probably right. I don't want to exclude my son from a holiday that we've spent together every year of his life. But I can't bear the thought of not sharing this first Christmas with Silas. And it would be damned awkward for the three of us to spend it together.

"Sorry, kiddo," I say. "It's a weird situation, I know."

Another huff, but it's closer to a laugh this time than a disgusted snort. "Understatement of the century, Dad."

I push the plunger on the French press down slowly and pour myself a cup of coffee. "So. Christmas with your mom, then," I say. "Sounds like a good time. I'll miss you, though." Which is true, despite everything.

"Yeah, I'll miss you too, Dad."

"Tell your mother Merry Christmas for me."

"I will. And, uh..." He clears his throat. "Same to Silas from me."

"I'll tell him," I promise. "Let me know when you get back."

"Will do, Dad. Love you."

"Love you, too, son."

Lance ends the call and I lay my phone facedown on the counter. So. That solves that problem.

I survey the pan on the stovetop and the egg carton I've taken from the fridge. You know what? Screw it. I put every-thing away, pour a second cup of coffee, doctor it with cream and sugar for Silas, and take both cups upstairs.

Silas is still a lump under the covers. I set the coffee cups on the nightstand, coil and stow away the ropes from last night, and climb onto the bed next to him.

I peel back the covers enough to expose an ear and bend close to blow gently across it. "Baby boy," I whisper, then lick at the shell of his ear. "Time to wake up."

"Nnnggh," Silas says into the space between the pillows and mattress. He doesn't turn over or open his eyes, but he does wiggle his ass toward me.

I worm my hand under the covers and grip a handful, squeezing his cheek hard enough to make him squeak. He opens his eyes and looks blearily over my shoulder.

"Good morning, sweetheart."

"Mmmphm," he grunts, then closes his eyes again. "Still dark outside."

"It's almost seven," I tell him. I'm usually up and dressed by now, getting ready to drive back to the city for the week. The sun's about to rise, though the dawn is obscured by gray clouds. We're due for a couple of inches of snow today, which is all the more reason to play hooky from work and go with my new plan for the day.

Silas's nose twitches. "Is that coffee I smell?"

I kiss the tip of his nose. "Mmm-hmm. Sit up and you can have some."

He squirms his ass into my hand instead and I squeeze him hard again. "You don't really want a spanking instead of coffee first thing in the morning, do you?"

He lets out a gigantic, put-upon sigh, but pushes himself upright and lets the covers fall into his lap. "No, Daddy."

He makes grabby hands toward the coffee and I hand it over to him, then settle my back against the headboard, my own coffee in hand. His hair is sticking up on one side and there's a pillow crease on his cheek. He's the most beautiful boy I've ever seen. And he's mine.

He takes a few sips of his coffee, then slumps down against the pillows, drawing his knees up and cradling the mug against his stomach. "I guess you have to go to work today, yeah?"

He looks utterly despondent, and it's not nice of me, but I can't help chuckling. "We'll have plenty of time to be together, sweetheart. You can't be jealous of my job."

He gives me a look from under his bangs. "Wanna bet?"

"I should punish you for your disrespect," I say mildly. Silas's morning wood twitches and I shake my head. "But, as it happens, I have other plans for us today."

Silas squirms out from under the covers and puts his coffee cup on the nightstand, then gets on all fours and waggles his ass in my direction. "Ooo, goody. Spankings? Tying me up again? Fucking me?"

I do smack his ass, though only once, and he rocks forward from the strength of it, then settles back with a low groan.

"We're going out for breakfast, then getting a Christmas tree."

Silas swings his head around quick enough to unbalance him and he lands on the cheek that I spanked. He winces, then lifts up and rubs it. "We're what?"

"Going out for breakfast, then getting a Christmas tree," I repeat. "There's a tree farm I go to every year."

"Wait, *out* for breakfast? Like in public? Together?"

"Of course. We can't spend the rest of our lives in bed." I reach for his cock and slide my fingers along the underside until his balls are cupped in my hand. "Might cage this, though, to remind you to behave."

Silas lets me fondle him, even as his eyebrows draw together. "A Christmas tree? Don't you usually wait until Christmas Eve to do that? With...um, Lance?"

I tell him about my conversation with Lance and how he's spending Christmas with his mother. "An opportunity to create some new traditions," I finish. "With my baby boy."

I tug him toward me and he comes forward willingly enough, even if his expression is still hesitant. I rest the hand holding my nearly-empty coffee mug on the pillow next to me and cup his face with my other hand. I kiss him until his face softens and his cock hardens, as does mine.

When Silas pulls back, his lips are puffy and wet and his eyes are shining. He squirms backwards a few feet and reaches for the waistband of my pants.

"We've got time for a little breakfast in bed first, though, right, Daddy?"

I let him take my cock out and position his parted lips just above the tip. He flicks his eyes up at me, waiting for permission, like a good boy.

My very good boy.

"Yes, baby," I say. And I give him everything he asks for.

Epilogue

SILAS

HOLY FUCKING SHIT, I can't believe this. I'm sitting in a center orchestra seat, in the third row, at the freaking Lyric Theatre, and it's opening night of my musical.

My musical. That I poured my heart and soul into writing. That James Cohen, who's about to take his seat in the row in front of me, took a chance on. He took a chance on me, an untried composer and lyricist, and poured a shocking amount of money into a production that I still haven't seen in its full glory.

I mean, I was present for all the initial meetings with the director and choreographer that James hired, and some of the meetings with the lighting and set designers. I've met the cast and most of the crew. I know the orchestra members really well and the conductor has been an absolute joy to work with.

I've seen parts of the dance numbers while Marcel Fontaine, the choreographer, worked out the steps. I've made changes to the score and the lyrics to account for technical issues that James and the director he hired convinced me were insurmountable the way I'd written them.

But as the show came together, I stopped attending rehearsals. It felt like, I dunno, tempting fate or something to be hanging around the theater the closer the show came to opening. I didn't even attend the previews, though Logan did.

Every show. For two solid weeks.

And speaking of Logan, he puts his hand on my knee, which has been bouncing pretty much since I sat down.

"I knew I should have caged you before we left the apartment." He leans close and whispers this in my ear and I can't tell whether it's his words or his breath tickling my ear or just the nearness of him that makes my dick stiffen under my tuxedo pants.

"Fuck, no," I whisper back. "I can't wear a cock cage to the freaking theater."

"You know it calms you down."

I doubt anything, even the cock cage, can calm me down tonight. And Logan's all talk, anyway. He'd never put me in the cage and then make me interact with an entire theater of people.

Well, except for that one time he did, when he took me to see *Harry Potter and the Cursed Child* for my birthday. And then fucked me bent over the kitchen island in his—now our—Upper West Side condo because he couldn't wait to take the extra steps into our bedroom.

He rubs his big hand soothingly up and down my thigh and dammit, maybe I should have let him cage me because his hand is having the opposite effect and my dick is all the way hard now.

"You're not helping," I hiss. I lay my Playbill on my lap to hide the bulge in my pants and shove Logan's hand off my thigh.

He chuckles next to my ear and I shiver. His efforts at distraction are working, though, at least temporarily. I'm not nervous anymore, just horny.

Until Logan settles back in the red velvet upholstered chair next to me and gestures at the stage. "It's going to be a hit, sweetheart," he says.

Of course he believes that. He's my Daddy, and it's his job to believe in my show. I'm still having trouble believing it myself, though.

In that uncanny way Logan has of reading my mind, he puts his arm around my shoulders. "James isn't worried at all, and you shouldn't be, either."

James is still holding court on the red carpet just in front of the stage, though the curtain's supposed to open in like, five minutes. A steady stream of well-dressed people swirl around him—investors, presumably, patrons and theater buffs, some of whom will probably be at the opening night party later. Oh god, some of these people could be critics. I'm going to puke.

Both Logan and James tried to show me the good reviews from the previews, but I refused to look at them. More superstition, I guess, but now I'm having a hard time remembering why I even wanted to do this in the first place.

Before I can lurch out of my seat and make a run for the john, the house lights dim momentarily and then brighten again. The international symbol for people to stop gabbing and find their seats. Shit. It's curtain time.

James exchanges air kisses with yet another older lady wearing a sequined dress and shakes hands with what must be her husband. Holy crap, do they know what they're in for with my show? They probably have season tickets and attend just about anything, but they're older than my parents, for fuck's sake. What are they going to think about a version of *Oedipus Rex* where the entire cast is queer and Thebes is the name of the spaceship they're on, not the Greek city in which the original play is set? And, oh my god, what about the scene with the tentacles?

My parents are here, too—several rows back but still in the center orchestra section—and Lance is somewhere in the theater, too, and they're all invited to the party after the show and suddenly it hits me anew that this theater seats nearly two thousand people, it's sold out, and everyone came here to see my musical.

"Easy, baby boy," Logan murmurs in my ear. "You're fine."

I'm really not. I'm bent nearly in half, trying to get my head between my knees, so I don't pass out, but the row in front of me is too close and I'm having trouble breathing. Logan strokes my back a few times, but it doesn't help.

"Sit up."

I obey immediately, because that's Daddy's voice—the command tone Logan uses mostly when we're alone, but which never fails to reach me, even in my absolute panic.

"I know you're nervous, Silas. But this show doesn't belong only to you anymore. A lot of people have put a lot of money and time into this show and it's ready. You know it is. You'll honor the work everyone's put into it and behave like the professional I know you are."

I turn to look at him and he gazes steadily back at me. He's also dressed in a tuxedo and the silver strands in his hair glint in the lights of this 1920s-inspired grand theater. He's so handsome it almost hurts to look at him and he's got that tiny smile playing around his lips that's only for me.

"Would I put you in a situation you can't handle?"

"No, Daddy," I whisper. People are settling in their seats around us, unwrapping scarves and flipping through their Playbills, so I think no one will hear me. I don't normally call him that outside our homes, but I need the reminder right now.

That Logan set all of this in motion because he believes in me and my work. But also that he's right—the show isn't just mine anymore. It belongs to James, who smiles at me when he finally takes his seat, and Marcel, who floats up the aisle in a confection of black silk and tulle wrapped around his lithe dancer's body, and perches lightly on the seat next to James.

And the rest of the team—the director, the lighting and set designers, the cast and crew. So many people who poured their talent and passion into bringing my show to this stage tonight.

I lean forward and press a kiss to Logan's cheek. His close beard tickles my lips, and I inhale the spicy, woodsy scent of the oil he uses to keep it soft.

"Thank you, Logan. For everything."

"It's my pleasure, baby boy," he murmurs, then grips my chin to brush his lips against mine. "Now, enjoy your show."

"Yes, Daddy," I mouth against his lips. I pull away before we get in trouble for public indecency and settle back in my seat. I take a deep breath in and let it out slowly. The frantic bat wings flapping in my stomach ease to something more like butterflies. A whole flock of them, still careening around, but I'm ready now.

Logan threads his fingers through mine and rests our clasped hands on his knee. The curtain rises to reveal a fantastic landscape dominated by vibrant, ever-shifting lights. The first notes I composed ring out in the hushed theater. Here we go.

Want more from *His Dad Will Do*? Join my newsletter and check out the bonus guide I've created with inspiration photos, links, and more! https://www.annakensing.com/his-dad-will-do-join

Silas and Logan's kinky adventures continue in This Ride Will Do. And book 2 of the Will Do series is My Dead Wife's Ex Will Do. *Fifteen years of avoidance. One week in paradise. A secret that refuses to stay buried.*

Acknowledgments

I'm usually very much a 'sense-of-place' writer. Some authors research so they can write, whereas I write so I can research. I love digging into the history of a place or getting inspired by a place I've visited to set a story there. In this book, you might have noticed that Logan and Silas don't actually leave the house until the epilogue. So, I didn't need to travel to Westport, Connecticut to figure out this story and I did all my research for it online. You can see photos of the house that inspired Logan's house—along with other…ahem… items I researched—in the bonus guide for His Dad Will Do, available when you sign up for my newsletter. https://www.annakensing.com/his-dad-will-do-join

As ever, the folks in Becca Syme's Writing Office made the writing process far less lonely. Thanks to Golden Angel for always just-in-time assistance; to my best writing pal, Carrie, for encouragement and tips; and my wife for dropping everything and helping me through a crisis I had just when I thought I'd finished the book. And to my cat, Olive (better known as the Moose), who I'm honestly convinced hangs out with me while I'm writing sexy scenes primarily because she's hoping I'll write her a snuff film featuring the dog, who she hates so hard. Giles already had a cameo in *Hard Chrome*, so this is the Moose's turn. Big thanks to my editor, Jen Sharon, for helpful feedback, and to Courtney for two excellent suggestions. And to you, dear readers, for peeping on Logan and Silas in all their dirty deeds. If you enjoyed His Dad Will Do, give us a review on Goodreads, BookBub, or your usual retailer, eh?

Will Do Series

Love doesn't wait for permission

His Dad Will Do

Revenge-banging a cheating ex-boyfriend's dad. His father is my Daddy now.

My Dead Wife's Ex Will Do

Fifteen years ago, Jason fell into bed with his wife's ex on the night of her funeral. He's avoided Victor ever since. Now their daughter's destination wedding has them trapped in paradise. Victor is done waiting. Jason is terrified wanting him will cost everything. But Victor might be worth burning it all down.

This Ride Will Do

I'm tied up in his trunk, headed off the map, and in way over my head. That's what I get for thinking this ride will do...

Hard Chrome

A second chance, small town romance with an age gap between a hot-tempered mechanic and a cool-as-a-cucumber lawyer, competence kink (on both sides), a 1955 Ford Thunderbird in need of restoration, meddling best friends (and former best friends), a cat named Simone and a dog named Giles, at least three hundred houseplants, and car sex.

About the Author

Anna Kensing writes steamy contemporary and paranormal historical romances that flirt with taboo. Her characters are often weird, mostly queer, and always get their happily-ever-after. Eventually.

She's obsessed with octopuses and the tv show *Supernatural*, listens to classical flute duets and heavy metal music while writing, and loves her scotch and Irish whiskies. When she's not thinking about writing, she's usually thinking about her next tattoo.

Sign up for her newsletter at https://www.annakensing.com